Never Odd or Even

"The book is a well-blended combination of elements: memoir, serio-comic escapades, pathos and full-rounded characterizations. None of the elements overrides the other and although a bittersweet tale, the story is never cloying. Some laugh-out-loud scenes and subtle good-natured satire devoid of bitterness. Subtly we see Charles mature and the black and white perception of his craft becomes more of a gray one. Deserves to do well."
                                                        —Bill Kelly

"*Never Odd or Even* is a delightful book, a tantalizing faux memoir of a brilliant career and the fascinating crimes that happened while making those films. Young delivers a story that's vivid, full of delightful character moments and shocking plot turns as his story unfolds in unexpected directions. In the end, it's about ambitions that are never quite realized and the accidental greatness we can create while our minds are on other things. It's also an absolutely page-turner that I couldn't put down."
                                                —Silver Bullet Jason

"Young delivers big laughs (at one point, Jerome is asked "to turn Joan Didion's collection of essays about the hippie culture of Haight-Ashbury into a... soap opera") and tight plotting. This is a good bet for Elmore Leonard fans."
                                                —*Publishers Weekly*

A CHARLES JEROME FILMOGRAPHY

Rotator (1960)

Was It a Cat I Saw? (1961)

Racecar (1962)

Summer and Sandy (1963)

No Room at The Royal (1964)

Tampico (1966)

Severance (1967)

Goin' Down (1969)

Slouching Towards Bethlehem (two-part TV movie; 1971)

Thorns in the Bed of Roses (1973)

The Borscht Belt (1974)

Central Casting (1975)

Biltmore 5-4500 (1977)

Carnations (1981)

Bitter Pills (1984)

Neon City (1988)

Blues of a Lifetime (1990)

12:04 (1994)

A Brief Episode (1997)

APO (2001)

Insecurities (2005)

A Minor Miracle (2009)

Never Odd or Even: The Film That Never Was
  (documentary; 2014)

In pre-production: *Never Odd or Even*
  (Showtime TV series)

NEVER ODD OR EVEN

FRANK M. YOUNG

Stark House Press • Eureka California

NEVER ODD OR EVEN

Published by Stark House Press
1315 H Street
Eureka, CA 95501
griffinskye3@sbcglobal.net
www.starkhousepress.com

ISBN: 979-8-88601-147-0

Cover and text design by Mark Shepard, shepgraphics.com
Proofreading by Bill Kelly

First Stark House Press Edition: June 2025

TO EMILY (WHO HAS READ THE BOOK)
AND CODY (WHO MIGHT SOMEDAY)

PROLOGUE

For too many years, when I had a moment between pictures, and when I got that mixed feeling of sentiment and horror, I drove crosstown to my storage facility. My unit, the size of a hall closet, cost me a monthly pittance. A heavy, rusted padlock protected its contents. The key, worn thin by years of fingering, still opened the lock. The metal complained as the bolt uncoupled and the door rumbled up. And there it was. Or, rather, *they*. There were two of them.

Two battered octagonal metal cans. Beneath their hinged lids were five reels of 35-millimeter black and white motion picture film. Each reel was banded with thick brown paper, secured with string wound around a red metal button.

To the rear of the space (which is five feet square) sat a large cedar chest. Inside were the elements that made up this movie. Negatives, an answer print, soundtrack stuff, everything but a shooting script.

I made this movie in the fall of 1962. You might know the other movie I directed then—a little character study called *Summer and Sandy*. It got a nod for Best Original Screenplay in the '64 Oscars and got me a Best Director nomination. It's the one I'll be remembered for—as much for the story about the film as the work itself.

I never wanted to make *Summer and Sandy*. I had another, more ambitious project in mind. That's the movie I come here to visit. Its title is scrawled in grease pencil on the two cans:

NEVER ODD OR EVEN

I'd love to show it to you. I've been working on getting that going. And I'm happy to say that it will happen. More about that later.

I'm a tough audience. In my youth, I was an arrogant SOB, and lashed out at films—even those I loved. Hitchcock, John Ford,

Casablanca, the Marx Brothers—it was all garbage, I proclaimed. I admired these films, and enjoyed them, but they weren't examples of what film could really achieve. They were all artifice—shot on soundstages, scored by massive orchestras, paid for by Hollywood studio moguls. They were made to make money. That any art came out of them is a happy accident.

Someone once asked me why I made films if I seemed to hate them so much. My reply: "I don't hate movies. I hate the system that compromises them. I hate that they're made with the idea of being a product. I hate that they don't reflect real life."

I went to film school (UCLA) and created three short films: *Racecar*, *Rotator* and *Was it a Cat I Saw? Racecar* won some awards, and you can find it on YouTube. All my student movies have palindromes for titles. Yes, I was a pretentious young man. But I did this with the idea that a movie should be completely self-contained; leave nothing untied, nothing implied. What you see, in my movies, is what you get.

Racecar was influenced by Robert Bresson. I'd seen *Pickpocket* and *A Man Escaped*, and learned that Bresson used non-actors, real locations, and despised artifice in a way that I could relate. That period of French film-making was a total inspiration to me. It disappointed me when I learned that *The 400 Blows*, Francois Truffaut's first feature, was shot silent, and that all the sound was non-diegetic. (There's a film-school word.) I loved the film's energy and freedom. I liked the idea behind *Breathless*, but like Jean-Luc Godard's other efforts, it seemed too arch, too coy.

The film that really killed me—my favorite film to this day—is *Los Olvidados*, shot in Mexico by Luis Buñuel. That is the movie by which I judge all other movies. I saw it for the first time in 1959, and I've never found another film that got to me so deeply, on so many levels. Anyone who doesn't like *Los Olvidados* is a stranger to me.

I hope you like it, because I'm about to spill my guts to you. Nobody lives forever, and I guess I want to get this off my chest. Clear the air. And maybe, if I tell my story right, you'll be able to see *Never Odd or Even*—the great work of my life—before too long.

ONE

I got the idea for *Never Odd or Even* from seeing *Gun Crazy*, an American independent movie released in 1949. A lot of it synced into the Hollywood film industry that I despised, but it had one sequence I watched over and over. It's a robbery scene filmed from the back seat of a car. The actors drive the car down a small-town street. The road is bumpy and the camera jerks and wobbles.

The robbery happens off-camera. The filming eye stays in the back seat, looking over the shoulder of Peggy Cummins, who plays one of the criminals. She sits there, waiting for the robbery to happen. An alarm sounds, and the man (John Dahl) dashes back to the car, panting and panicky. The car drives off and whips through side streets to elude the slow-witted law that only just reacted to the crime.

Of course, they get caught by film's end, in a spectacular studio set of a foggy mountain top—movie artifice at its most expressive and effective. But when I watch the finale, I'm constantly reminded that I'm looking at a made-up story, in a made-up environment where every square inch is controlled and planned.

That robbery sequence I could watch for three hours. Like the sun-bleached village streets of *Los Olvidados*, it just plain gets to me.

Due to *Racecar*'s success, and its warm reception (it got a nice notice by Bosley Crowther in the New York *Times*), I was courted by a few film studios. M-G-M asked me if I would consider expanding the 18-minute film to a feature in Technicolor—only this time with a professional cast, and shot their way, on their terms. I shook their hands, thanked them and politely turned them down.

Crown International was on the lower rungs of the film industry. They released grindhouse crap—drive-in stuff—but Newton Jacobs really liked what he'd heard about *Racecar* and invited me to screen my films for him.

I met him at Crown International's offices in Beverly Hills. It was a classy address for a company that thrust junk into the world. The secretary introduced herself as Magda, which I misheard as "magma." I waited in the tiny lobby and wondered if I looked the part of a serious film-maker in my Penney's three-button sports coat, thin striped tie and white unironed dress shirt.

Newton appeared. "Mister Jerome." We shook hands and he ushered me to his screening room. Someone had picked up prints of the three short films from UCLA. The first one, *Rotator*, was threaded up in the projector, ready to run.

"You haven't seen this film, Mr. Jacobs . . ."

"Newton. And no, sir, I haven't. An airplane picture?"

"Not, uh, really." I gave him a quick rundown of *Rotator*.

There used to be a potato chip factory out on Crenshaw Boulevard. It had a huge ventilator fan that must have been broken. Its metal blades turned slowly, night and day. The immediate neighborhood smelled of fryer oil and rancid fats.

The fan side of the building had a good view of a busy street and some of the downtown skyline. I wondered what life would look like to those fan blades as they poked their way around an unending circle of movement.

I got the idea to tie a film camera to it and let it photograph the nearby buildings and cars in a slow, constant loop, upside-down and right-side-up.

I did this over a period of six months, for the length of a magazine of 16mm film, in all different kinds of weather, and in black and white and color, depending on the film stock I had on hand. I edited it down to six minutes and 33 seconds. A jazz pianist friend composed a score for it, and I superimposed snippets of conversation, stuff recorded off my TV, sounds of city streets and the ocean.

It made some people sick to their stomachs, but enough liked it to earn a couple of awards in minor film festivals. I can't watch it anymore—it really *does* make me sick, all that whirling—but I think the musical score is lovely, and though it goes against my already-stated principles of realism, it's an interesting experiment.

"Interesting." Newton sounded neutral. "Not really what we're looking for here, but . . . interesting."

Was it a Cat I Saw? was next. This film hewed to my ethos. It's a fixed shot of the exterior of a house at night. Through two lit windows, we see and hear a young married couple in silhouettes against the curtains and shades. They talk about their day—he works in an insurance office, she at an elementary school—and the question that makes the film's title comes as a kind of ironic, funny-sad punchline to this overheard discussion. The pause, after that question is asked, and before one light, then the other, is turned off, either got uproarious laughter and applause or befuddlement, depending on the audience.

Newton laughed. And clapped. "I've had times like that with my wife. It's almost like you filmed us at home. Pretty clever." He straightened his tie. "Not really what we're looking for here, but . . . clever."

The projectionist saved *Racecar* for the finale. Shot in color at Venice Beach, *Racecar* was my attempt to do a Bresson. The star of the film was a fellow I spotted in line at Pink's, ordering a chili dog and an orange soda. At the risk of social embarrassment, I introduced myself to him. He had a look that inspired a film. He wasn't movie-star handsome—thank God—but he had something riveting that I knew would translate to celluloid.

He wasn't put off by my approach. "I make movies. You like movies?"

"What kind?" He got all shy.

"Art movies, I guess you could call them." And then added: "Not *that* kind of art movie. Movies about . . . life . . . real things human beings can relate to."

"Oh." His chili dog started to ooze off the limp paper plate. "Wanna siddown?"

I got a couple of dogs and we had lunch there on the sidewalk. He mentioned his name (which I forgot; I'm terrible with names) and that he was just out of high school, trying to figure out what came next in his life.

I explained my idea for the movie. There was a beautiful red Alfa Romeo Disco Volante in Venice Beach. It sat in a vacant lot beside a rusted sheet metal shed littered with tools, rags and grease. This car had run in some big races but had terrible engine problems.

The owner of the Alfa Romeo, who'd had it shipped from Europe, was told it couldn't run again. I would imagine you could just pop a new engine in it and, literally, be off to the races, but I'm not a car guy. Its owner seemed determined that he could fix it, given time and patience enough.

I'd talked with this guy. His name was Hank or Frank something, and he was retired. His idea of a good time was getting filthy dirty as he tinkered with this prize car. This was a project without end, and my brief talk with Hank or Frank left me with an idea.

I kept rolling it around. Didn't we all know a person like Hank or Frank? Someone who wanted to achieve a goal, and who clearly didn't have the means to achieve it, but was so taken with the idea that he couldn't do anything else? Hank or Frank spent his evenings at work on the car, while his wife and friends protested. He just chuckled. "They don't get it. Hand me that spanner? What, I should collect stamps? Or go to museums? Hell with that. No, this ain't the spanner, buddy."

He got it himself. Then he forgot I was there. This endless fussing and fiddling was what life was all about to him. The rest of it, including me, was just a botheration.

I had made a second visit to Hank or Frank, mentioned my vague idea for a movie, and asked if I could pay for some time to film an actor working on the car.

Hank or Frank looked upset. "What's he gonna do?"

"Nothing. You know how it is in movies. A person looks like he's doing something but he's not. I just like the image of this Alfa Romeo, sitting here, and I think I can do a nice movie about it."

"Just don't put me in it. I ain't no actor."

Turned out Hank or Frank volunteered at a blood bank most mornings and played squash in the afternoon. He spent his evenings diddling with the Alfa. So, the deck was clear until six each day. I gave him 100 dollars and he handwrote an agreement on the back of a receipt for an alternator.

Now I had an idea—a vague idea—and a great location. I needed people to do something with both.

Between bites of whatever part of whatever animal makes up a hot dog, I told the vague idea to the kid. He nodded and uh-huhed as I spoke.

"I'm not looking for a Marlon Brando. Just a person who can be themselves. I don't want you to act. I'll suggest what you might do, but I don't want anything to seem like it's planned. Almost like I'm filming something that's really happening. You dig?" He nodded, his cheeks full of chili dog.

"So. D'you know anything about cars . . .?"

"Eugene," he reminded me. "Little bit. 'Bout enough to change the spark plugs. I ain't no mechanic."

"Do you like cars?"

Eugene shrugged and smiled. "Guess I do. I sure do like a fast car."

"Could you see yourself doing this role? Just working on this car night and day? Not knowing if it would ever run again?"

Again, he shrugged. "Guess so." He paused for a mouthful of chili dog. Red sauce dribbled on his chin. "What's it pay?"

I scraped up 300 dollars, which he agreed to, and we shot the film over the summer. I found a woman to play his wife at Safeway. Virginia was a checkout clerk whom I'd talked up, with the dim idea that I'd ask her out. But it never got anywhere. She had an intelligence in her eyes that I thought would show up on the screen.

I caught her on a break and gave her the spiel that had won Eugene. She laughed. "I'm not an actress."

"I don't want an actress. I want *you*. Who you are. Nothing pretend."

She stalled again, and I mentioned that the role was good for 200 dollars. And all she had to do was be there in front of the camera. "No nude scenes, nothing like that. Just . . . get into the situation and act like you think you should. It won't be hard."

There *was* a script. I wrote it to get writing a script out of my system. I knew that the story and setting would drive everything else. I had some suggestions for where the story might go, but I was open to chance. That was part of real life. You don't go by a script. You wake up and hope for the best. You might get hit by a truck or win a million bucks. You never know.

The one bit of *Racecar* that was planned started out the film. Eugene stood at the big newsstand on Cherokee, in North Hollywood, and paged through the car magazines. We lucked out. A big British mag had a spread on the Disco Volante and its role in racing history. It seemed to interest him, and I got some great shots, including the stand manager advising him to buy the car magazine or move on.

Artie Sellon was my sound man on the picture, with a clunky reel-to-reel on his shoulder to get the audio. We'd braved the UCLA film program together and we liked just enough of the same movies to form a friendship.

I doubled as cameraman. Stupid, in retrospect, given Artie's skill as a DP, but I was into that total filmmaker malarkey back then. I wanted to do everything, and it pissed me off that I had to enlist other people.

For the Venice Beach sequences, a third student filmmaker, Thomas something, was assistant director and did the slate.

We had a basic premise—a guy who's in love with an impossible dream, and his woman, who tries to cope but can't compete with the car. Eugene was at first wooden and unresponsive, and we burned through many reels of color 16mm film before he warmed up and got into his character (which was himself.)

Virginia was great. She had a natural knack for generating real-world talk, and she became the girlfriend (or wife; the film never made this clear) who is in love with Eugene and wants so much to understand him and to take part in his dream.

As the two actors got to know each other, the dialogue was all improvised. I didn't make suggestions; just rolled the camera and sound. Virginia had an aunt who was dying of leukemia, and she brought that into the story. There's a terrific scene where she tells Eugene that this might be the last time he'll ever get to see this aunt alive, and that it's important to her that he go with her to say his farewell.

Eugene looks up, grief in his eyes. "I can't help her stay alive," he says, almost ashamed of himself. "I can bring *her* (the Alfa Romeo) back. I can't leave *her*."

To heighten the realism, Eugene and Virginia became romantically involved, then uninvolved, during the filming. The tension from their relationship brought more stakes to this simple story—something I hadn't thought out in detail, just an impulse, an idea based on the object, its location and the convenience that its name was a palindrome. It was a gift from the universe. On the final day of filming, during the last scene, when Virginia accuses Eugene of being a fool and tells him she's going to leave him— "all you love is this pile of junk! Not me!"—the blinding sunshine of Venice Beach clouded over, and rain dumped from the skies.

On cue, Virginia walked away, seeking shelter from the rain. One of her shoes fell off her feet and she splashed across the puddled street. Eugene stood by the car and said, to himself, "She could still run." And back to his work he went, absorbed by the rain. Fade to black.

I couldn't take credit for the dialogue. Life and chance had written the ending for me. My credit was "filmed by Charles Jerome." The actors got credit for the dialogue; I gave myself credit for the general idea of the film.

At 18 minutes, *Racecar* said everything it could say. Aside from some wild sequences of Eugene and Virginia strolling the beachfront, with all its nutjobs, and the newsstand bit at the beginning, all the action took place in the open field where the car sat.

From its first screening, *Racecar* generated a buzz. Other students asked me where I'd found such good actors. "From real life," I said. My major professor was moved by the film. "You've *got* something here. I wouldn't know what to call it, but you've *got* something here."

All I did was pick two people, a compelling location and an object, and let the world take its course. I guided it here and there, but I tried to keep every moment, every gesture as real and simple as I could. I resisted the inclination to do arty camera angles. I moved the camera from spot to spot, to give some visual variety, but no viewpoint was something you wouldn't see if you were standing there in the field.

When Variety did a piece on *Racecar*, mentioning its notoriety at film festivals and its new style of realism, doors opened for me. Most of those doors weren't the ones I wanted open, but I went through them, met people and thanked them for their interest.

I didn't want to make *Racecar* again. That was done. I wanted to build on what I'd achieved with the film—half happy accident, half purposeful choice. But whomever I worked for—or with—had to get that about me. They had to really understand *Racecar*.

Newton got it. The lights came up and he looked lost in thought. He wiped his eyes—from tears?—and turned to me. *"This."* He gestured to the blank screen. "This *told* me something. It showed me what life is really about. What we're all trying to find while we're alive."

"Thank you, Newton."

"No. Thank *you*." He patted my shoulder.

We left the screening room. Down the hallway was his office. He showed me in. Over bourbons, Newton Jacobs gave me carte blanche. I'd have to finance my own production, but if it had marquee value—any theme that would draw an audience— he'd be proud to release it.

Over our drinks, I told him about how much I liked *Gun Crazy*, and that movies about crime seemed like a sure-fire genre. He agreed. "Just keep all that psychological crap out of it," Newton warned me. "All that does is confuse people." He mentioned a movie that I recognized as *The Killing*, Stanley Kubrick's early effort. I admired the movie, but I could never feel comfortable darting around in time as Kubrick did.

On a handshake, with the stipulation that I had to foot the bill for my production, get it ready for release and then offer it to Crown, it was a done deal that they'd release it.

I walked out into the late afternoon sun and felt like a king. If this movie did well at the box office, I'd stand to make more money on it than through the traditional studio system. I was sick of peanut butter and baked beans, and the thought that I might turn my art into something that could sustain and nurture me was a powerful possibility.

And, most important to me, I'd get to make a movie that felt real. Everything in it would happen in actual places, move through real spaces, and nothing would distract the viewer with artifice. When a car drove down the road, there would be real road moving into the distance and the dark. Woods would be woods, not some fairy-tale forest assembled by salaried artisans. Every stick, bug and dust speck in this film would be the real deal.

Now all I needed was a story. A crime story. Nothing complicated or obtuse. And something I wanted to make. *I'll base it on a book*, I thought. I recalled how Orson Welles took a paperback potboiler and turned it into *Touch of Evil*, a baroque movie with moments of real brilliance. Welles was a little too in love with himself for me, but I got where he was coming from.

I drove to an all-night drugstore, spun the paperback carousel, and grabbed the first book I touched. It was a diet book for expectant mothers. No box office there. I spun again. I got a science fiction story—one of those cerebral affairs with abstract cover art. Nope.

Third time lucky. The moment I saw the cover, I knew this was it.

EVERYTHING HE TOUCHED WAS GOLD—
OR WAS IT?
The Story of a Desperate Man in
A Town Without a Soul!
NEVER ODD OR EVEN
An original Beacon novel by OTIS C. KENTON

The cover painting showed a smoky, claustrophobic room. Scowling faces frame a green felt table. In the center, hunched forward, a haunted, sweaty man throws the dice. The red cubes linger in the foreground, forever frozen in a 3-D moment of expectation. In the background, a sultry brunette looks on with either desire or disinterest. Part of the cover text obscured her eyes, so I couldn't tell.

I hadn't read a word of this book. And why should I? This was going to be my first feature film. A movie that would set the film industry on its ears. Show them they were in the dark ages. Be a beacon, if you will, to a better way of making movies.

I shoplifted the book and headed home. My heart raced as I drove.

I parked by the ocean and watched the night waves foam and thrash. The air smelled of salt and my head was on fire.

I took the book from my coat pocket, kissed it for good luck, and tossed it into the waves. They took it away and I went home. I fell into fell into a sweet, restful sleep.

TWO

In the morning, over my first cup of coffee and a cigarette, I sat in the sunlight at my kitchen table. The smoke swirled into the dusty light and lingered before me. I had a start for a movie. The world had dropped it into my lap. Now all I needed was an idea.

And so I sat. And sat. And nothing showed up.

Hunger got me out of this limbo. I took a quick shower and walked down to the corner. Some eggs and toast (and more coffee) at the drugstore café helped me perk up. The beginning of a project is always like this. You have the germ of a great idea—that's half the battle won. If you can make anything out of it, there's the victory.

Maybe I was exhausted from the day before. A lot had happened. My head felt heavy, like it was trying to work beyond its ability.

A metal squeak snapped me out of my head. A couple of kids were at the drugstore's paperback carousel. They found a *Mad* collection and cackled. My eye went to a copy of *Never Odd or Even*.

I was close enough that I could just reach the carousel. I pulled the book out with two fingers. I looked at the cover again. Got absorbed in the scene.

Okay. I'll read the book. Fine. I'll even pay for it this time. I settled up and walked back to my apartment. I flipped through the book. It was 192 pages. I had nothing on my agenda. I could read this in one sitting.

I sprawled out on my couch and read the come-on page, just inside the front cover:

> "I have to win—or I'm dead!"
>
> Charlie Jerome had a way with the dice. He called them his "dancing girls." He staked everything on this game—his wealth, his love and his life.
>
> If he lost, Vinnie Boroni would see to it that he was pushing

up daisies—fast!

If he won, he'd be set for life. And he'd have Belinda. Only the "dancing girls" knew his fate—and they weren't talking!

Las Vegas, with its glitz and glamour, is the setting for this original BEACON novel by Otis C. Kenton, author of STREET TRASH and A KITTEN IN HELL.

Yes, I was spooked by the main character's name. Another of life's coincidences, and further proof that I was on the right track. I flipped to the first chapter and read.

I'd like to say that *Never Odd or Even* (the book) was a pulp masterpiece. It was better than I expected but fell short of its potential. Otis C. Kenton had a good eye for detail. He made you feel like you were in Las Vegas. If he left out one synonym for *hot* or *sweaty,* I missed it. His descriptions of the gambling atmosphere painted a strong picture. But he rushed through things and didn't explain enough to make me care about Charlie Jerome.

The book would have made a decent normal picture. I could see the Hollywood ending tacked on to the novel's fatal climax. Charlie Jerome wouldn't fall to the ground dead, as he does in the book. Belinda, played by, say, Jayne Mansfield, would pick him up before he fell, and he'd confess that he was a fool, and that if she'd only love him, he'd straighten up, and get a job, and be a good guy. And Belinda, of course, would say "Ya idiot, don't ya know I've always loved you?"

Then the camera would cut to a reverse shot. They'd walk into the light of a new day, down the trash-strewn street, and the music would swell and those words I hate—and have never put on my films—would pop up:

THE END

Of course, it's the end! People don't need to be told this. Those are the two most depressing words in the world. Nothing ever ends. It atrophies; it decays; it dies. But it never truly ceases to be.

Enough of that. I'd read the book. It had nothing I wanted except the title.

I wrote the managing editor of Beacon Books with an inquiry about movie rights for *Never Odd or Even*. He replied a week later: *Is this a joke?*

I assured him I was on the level. I wanted to make a movie based on the Otis C. Kenton Beacon paperback original *Never Odd or Even*. He could name a price and we could negotiate. He could take the money and run. I enclosed the clipping from *Variety* (I'd bought 10 copies) about *Racecar* and its festival success. He replied five days later via airmail. He asked if he could get 10% of the film's gross, in exchange for his saying yes.

I sent him a telegram:

AGREED TEN PERCENT OF FILM GROSS. DO YOU WANT TO SIGN AN AGREEMENT? JEROME

The guy called me. The cross-continent connection was rotten. "Mister Jerome? I got your wire."

"Yes." The line crackled in silence.

"This is legit? You're serious?"

"Yes."

"It's just . . . no one's ever wanted to make a movie out of a Beacon book." The line hissed. "I never thought anyone really *read* 'em." Another pause. "So what did you *like* about it?"

"The title."

"The *title*."

"It's a great title. Not a bad book, but the title's a keeper."

"The *title*."

"I might use some of the scenes in the book, but the film's story is going to be different. Not about gambling."

"*Not* about gambling." The line hummed. "Then what's it going to be *about*?"

"To be honest, Mr. . . ."

"Crohn."

"To be honest, Mr. Crohn, I'm not 100 percent sure. But I assure you it will be a good picture. One Beacon Books can be proud of."

"Beacon Books can never be proud of *anything*, Mr. Jerome."

Crohn chuckled. "Well. You make your picture, then get in touch with me. You want to cut me in on the percentages, fine. But you're cutting *me* in—not Beacon Books." Either the static got louder, or he was whispering. "They're with the ob-may."

"Mafia?"

"No no *no*. Don't say that word. We don't *use* that word around here."

I agreed. Crohn (I never did get his first name, but he never did get any money) would get a piece of the *Never Odd or Even* pie, once it was out of the oven. I bid him adieu. It was about five. I had the rights to the book. To the title.

Now I had to build a movie around those four words.

THREE

Though I'd graduated from UCLA, I still had access to their facilities. I used them to screen all the bank heist movies I could track down. Some went back to the early days of the talkies. All of them had their moments, but none satisfied me. I kept going back to that sequence in *Gun Crazy*—its realism and tension killed me every time I watched it.

I wanted a whole movie with that feel. I wanted the audience to believe that these crimes were unfolding in their lap—that the people on screen were honest-to-God hoodlums, desperate and lawless. I would show the life and world of the criminal like no one had ever gotten it before.

But what did I know from crime? I'd shoplifted—sometimes due to forgetting to pay for a candy bar, a magazine, cigarettes—but I had no deep-set tendencies. I wasn't a Dillinger. And I couldn't make this movie unless I had some understanding of that life.

"So, you're gonna rob a bank?" Artie Sellon laughed into his coffee cup.

"Well . . . maybe. If there's no other way." I sipped my coffee. We sat in the drugstore café as I laid out my ideas for *Never Odd or Even* from notes scrawled on a yellow legal pad. My brain was a mess. I had to talk my ideas out, get a firm grasp on them before they slipped away.

"So, what? We're just gonna make it all up? You doin' a screenplay?"

"Maybe just a treatment. Something we can work from. We can agree that such-and-such is going to happen, and how it happens is up to chance."

"They got books about crime. Studies."

"Yeah." I had a stack of case studies of career criminals from the college library. They were dry. Hard to believe something so interesting could become so damned dull!

"Refill?" Artie said, too loud. He had—and still has—a nasal voice that grates. I saw the waitress wince. She scowled as she approached us.

"Regular or unleaded?" Without waiting for the answer, she refilled our mugs.

"Everyone's a comedian." Artie sipped his too-hot coffee.

"Maybe I could meet a real criminal. Wouldn't that be great? Hear about how they do it. Nothing made up. Just the day-to-day life of a bank robber."

"Good luck finding this person or persons." Artie picked at his apple pie. That was better than eating it.

Long story short: Artie liked the vague idea I had. He agreed that a crime picture with convincing realism—no Hollywood moments—was a strong idea. But could it be done? How could I learn enough about criminal life to get the right voice?

I didn't know. Artie had a date and was worried he'd be late. I walked home, and for a few minutes I fell into a funk. What did I know about this side of life? I was a sheltered kid. My folks had money. I didn't want for anything. I'd never *had* to steal. That's what I had to learn. *Why* someone wants to steal what isn't theirs. Not for a thrill, like I did as a kid, but as a matter of life or death.

I felt fed up when I got home. I paced my living room, kicked the sofa a couple of times, turned on the TV, changed channels, shut it off and stood in the silence of early evening. I heard traffic sounds drift up the airshaft in the bathroom. The sounds of people who didn't have the problems I had.

No, that wasn't right. We all have our cross to bear. We worry how we're going to pay the light bill. Whether the girl (or boy) of our dreams will ever show up—and, if they do, whether they really could love us back. Whether we'll get that raise, that job, that vacation.

I paced and thought faster. *This* is what drives us all. And what makes some of us take desperate measures to solve our problems. Maybe some people can't cope with the pressure. They lack the faith that things will sort themselves out. And so, they take a harder route to get what they need. Their anxiety—and fear—

pushes them away from reality.

Yes, this was it. It worked on an intellectual level. What little I'd read seemed to back this notion up. But how could I prove it was right?

I was out of smokes. (I quit that rotten habit years later, I'm proud to say.) I grabbed my coat and went out. Night was here and the street in front of my apartment building was full of life. Couples headed to a nice dinner, a movie, a future pregnancy. Cars, cars, cars. Including mine, which I saw down the street. I got closer and I saw him. A silhouette at first. Someone trying the door, opening it . . .

I broke into a fast walk. The silhouette had the door open on the passenger's side. I always forgot to lock it. He leaned under the steering wheel.

No one else seemed to notice him. I got within 10 feet of my car. The figure took shape and form. Blue jeans with frayed cuffs; worn work boots. I steeled myself for a confrontation. "*Excuse* me."

He didn't hear me. "Excuse me. *Hey*. That's my car."

The figure startled and smacked his head hard on the underside of the steering wheel. I thought he had knocked himself out. "Hey. You still alive?"

He stirred, swore and turned so I got a good look at him. He was maybe two years older than me. His tired, taut face had dark patches under his eyes. I could tell he hadn't bathed—maybe not for a week. He looked like he belonged in one of those "daring" pictures about degeneracy in the deep South. "Who th' fuck're you?"

"The guy who owns this car."

He squinted as he took this in. His shoulders slumped. "Awright. I'm it. Yuh got me."

I waited a moment. He fidgeted, as if my next move would slay him. "I'm not gonna call the cops."

He looked half-way up—not ready to meet my eyes. "No?"

"You hungry?" He nodded. "Come on. Let's go to Hody's." I gestured to the open passenger door. He looked up at me, still surprised by this turn of events. But he sat down, and off to Hody's we went.

WE LOVE YOUR CHILDREN, a banner read as I parked in the

Hody's lot at La Brea. At the height of dinnertime, there were plenty of children to love—or hate—screaming, spilling and whining in the bright-lit booths.

We got a small booth and waited for service. "My name's Charles."

He looked at me with suspicion. "Hey, I ain't that kinda guy."

It took me a moment to get what he said. "No, I'm not wanting that. But I am wanting something. If you're willing to give it to me."

A waitress forced a dramatic pause in our conversation.

"Get whatever you want," I told my new friend.

"Really?"

I nodded, and he ordered a full meal. I went for a club sandwich and coffee.

"So, whud'ja *wawnt?*" He talked like an Okie; I could imagine him in *The Grapes of Wrath*, doing a scene with John Carradine. I told him everything you know so far. If he would talk to me about his life of crime, help me to understand why someone chooses this life, I'd be able to make my movie—and there'd be a part in it for him. Who better to play a criminal? Not some laid-back pretty-boy or earnest Broadway import. A real down to-earth human being.

Over our Hody's meal (and the braying of a million beloved children), he told me his name—Sam Mellinger—and his life story. He never knew his parents. They were sent to jail for grand larceny when he was four. He grew up in a series of foster homes in Oklahoma. His childhood sounded like hell. Just the growing up in Oklahoma part gave me the chills. "They gimme jussa nuff food t' stay alive. And then they work me from sun up t' midnight. And you hadda wartch your back. Them older boys'd kill ya soon as look atcha."

Sam ran away from his last foster home at 15 and hitched a series of rides to Los Angeles. He lived off the streets. He tried to hold up a bottle shop on Sepulveda and found himself on the wrong end of a shotgun. The cops put him in a work home, which was a step up from foster life. "Lease ya knew what you was in for there. Long's ya did y'r work 'n didn't make trouble, you could do okay."

As Sam talked, I thought of my youth, in contrast. While he worried about getting killed in his sleep, I was mortified because I had braces. I complained about what I didn't have—which was nothing, really—and Sam took whatever life offered him and was grateful. It was hard to relate to his way of life, but I had to learn.

"Fine'ly got out uh the work home. I was 18. I got me a job workin' on cars. Did perty good at it, but in about a year the boss got a gold ring stole. I wadn't even there when it happened, but they blamed me and gimme the sack." He stopped to take in a mouthful of steak. He ate like a dog—as if all food would cease to exist if he slowed down.

"What did you do then?" I nibbled on my sandwich.

"Got another job. Then another. Warshin' dishes, pumpin' gas, d'liverin' appliances. That was the lass honest job I ever had. An the one that started me in thinkin' 'bout life."

"Yeah?"

"Me an' this other guy, we'd be goin' into these rich people's homes every day, puttin' in their new dish-warshers, stoves 'n whutnot. An' they had all this fancy stuff just lyin' around. I'd see jool'ry, money clips, silverware, none of it locked up, just sayin' *take me, c'mon Sam, take me.* I was gettin' three bucks a day t' bust my ass slingin' these heavy crates, an' I fine'ly listened to what them things was sayin'."

Sam had seen enough crime movies to know he had to think this out. He staggered his breaking-and-entering capers a week or two after a delivery. Sometimes he'd luck out—a window was unlocked, or open, and no one was around. "People don't pay 'tension to nothing but themselves. Long as you're keerful, you c'n git away with anything."

He learned to take a clipboard—stolen from the appliance store— a pocket flashlight, and to dress up, as best he could. If questions were asked, he had an instant reason for being there. He was stopped by cops twice—each time after he'd successfully cleaned out a house of its goodies. "They was just talkin' to me, tellin' me to be keerful, an' me with gold an' whatnot in my pockets." Sam laughed at the memory.

"So how is a life of crime treating you?"

Sam startled at my words, and looked around, in case Broderick Crawford was on his trail. He smiled and shrugged. "Purty good. It's what-you-call . . . famine or feast. Yuh have a good run, then it all dries up. People stort to lock their doors. For a while. You hafta wait it out, let 'em drop their guard, an' then the fun storts all over again."

He broke into a broad grin. I had to smile too.

We fell into silence. Sam wolfed the rest of his steak and ignored his green beans. I finished my sandwich and held my empty coffee cup so the waitress could attend to it. After the refill, Sam looked up at me. A wad of steak bulged in one cheek. "You wawna taste of it?"

"I'm okay. You finish it."

He swallowed. "Ain't whut I mean. You wawna see what it's like?" He looked to his left, then right. "What I do?"

I never thought about this angle. I felt scared and thrilled. I took a sip of coffee. "Of course. When?"

He smiled. Steak was stuck between his teeth. "You settle our bill 'n' I'll show ya."

I settled our bill. Sam chewed and swallowed, chewed and swallowed. He finished his coffee and we left the lovable children to wreak their havoc at Hody's. I got a glimpse of a bawling little girl covered in cling peach slices and drooling syrup.

We got to my car. I unlocked the doors. "So . . ."

"You drive. I'll fine us a good spot." I started the engine and we cruised out to the Silverlake area—winding streets of comfortable homes. "'S Friday night," Sam said, after a long silence. "Been a long week. Mom don't feel like cookin' dinner, 'n' Dad wants t'have too many martinis. So, they go out fer the night. Nice meal, see a movie, play cords with friends. Don't matter what they do. Long'zey leave their house for us."

We drove down a quiet street. Sam scanned the passing houses for a likely prospect. "Go on down to the end of the block an' park."

I parked under a tree and shut off the engine. The quiet struck me. If you strained, you could hear the freeway traffic, but you had to work at it. The rustle of leaves in the night wind, some bird songs and the muted jabber of television gave this crowded, go-getter city a sense of calm.

"Less walk around." Sam and I were careful to not slam the car doors. "Walk soft," he whispered. He had a way of moving his feet that made no sound. I couldn't do it. He padded across an immaculate lawn and onto the pavement. I felt like a horse, clomping and kicking as I tried to match his quiet.

I caught up with him. "What are we looking for?"

"We'll know it when we find it." He surveyed the houses. "TV's on—nope . . . Lights out but there's two cars in the driveway. Pro'lly early risers . . ." The third house was in the middle of a party. Modern jazz blared from a hi-fi, glasses tinkled, and laughter fluttered from the screen door of a split-level ranch house. Sam dismissed them with a disgusted sound. Then he alerted, like the forest animals in Walt Disney's *Bambi* when the big fire starts.

I heard the hissing of tires. A cop car pulled alongside us. Some neighbor must have called them and complained that someone else was having too much fun.

"Lousy party," Sam said, loud and clear. "Too damn noisy for me."

"Yeah, gives me a headache. I'm glad we left."

"Evenin', awff'cers." Sam turned his head. The cop car stopped.

A collegiate crewcut type, dressed in patrolman black, walked towards us. He waggled a flashlight beam in our general direction. "You fellas at that party?"

"We *were*." I smiled and tried not to look tipsy. "Nothin' goin' there, officer, believe me. Just a lotta hot air."

"An' mortinis," Sam added.

College boy laughed. "You know the Ronsons?"

"Kind of. We got invited by one of their friends."

"They're nice people," Sam slurred. "A li'l bit in their cups t'night."

Joe College grinned. "Yeah, they get that way on the weekends. We always get a call 'bout 'em." He clicked off his flashlight. He stopped, hands on hips, and surveyed the whooping jazz and forced guffaws. "Gee, I hate to . . . say, fellas, would you mind?"

"Huh?"

"Could you go back and ask 'em to keep it down, just a little? I know they're tired of seeing me show up."

I shrugged. Sam shrugged back. "I could use one for the road." I looked at college boy and pointed at Sam. "*He's* driving."

The cop grinned. "Just keep your noses clean, fellas. Have a good evening."

"Night." The cop car hissed away from us.

"So . . ." I looked at Sam.

"Y'know, this is a whole new angle. I gotta idea."

We stopped at the street in front of the party house. The Ronsons had a novelty mailbox. It was a miniature log cabin with HERB AND BARB RONSON'S painted in rustic letters.

We walked into Herb and Barb Ronson's living room. Twenty suburbanites, the youngest in their mid-20s, drank, smoked and gabbed. "We're *back*!" Sam grinned like a hyena.

"And we're *thirsty*!" I shouted. Everyone smiled.

A portly, balding guy with black horn-rims beckoned us over. "Can't have thirst on the premises. What'll it be, gents?"

"Vodka tonic for me." I looked at Sam. "What's your weakness?"

"Bourbon neat."

"Easy orders. I'm Herb."

"Rick," I said. "This is Morty."

"Shorty Morty and Slick Rick," Herb said. He howled at his own joke. He had to make a noise every 10 seconds—a cough, sniffle or cackle—to remind the world he was alive. Between hand flourishes, snippets of Perry Como and Dean Martin songs and general banter about suburban life, he juggled bottles, glasses, jars and ice tongs.

He made great drinks. They could peel layers of paint off a stone wall. I sipped mine and swallowed hard. "Make yourselves comfy, gents. There's pizza pie in the dining room. From Shakey's."

We feigned interest and he led us in. "We couldn't hire the fellas who sing, but the pizza's good." We each got a slice and nibbled. "So where do I know you . . . Rick?"

"That's it, Herb. I know I've seen *you* before. What line of work you in?"

He beamed. "Best there is, buddy. The real estate game. Houses, townhomes, businesses . . ."

"*That's* where I know you!" I would have snapped my fingers, were I able. "You showed me a beautiful place out in the Canyon .

. . ." I crumpled my brow, waiting for him to finish my thought.

"The Don DeFore house!" He swigged his amber alcohol. "Too bad, buddy. That place was a steal!"

"Yeah. By the time I asked the wife about it, it was gone." I plowed more pizza in my mouth.

"What a commission I got from that sale!" Herb straightened his horn-rims. "Hate to brag, Rick, but the real estate game is the best racket in town. Sometimes I feel like a crook! But I make people happy. I sell 'em dreams. It's up to them to take that dream and make it come true. But I sure do sell 'em a grade-A dream!"

"When I get back from Europe, I'll look you up."

"Where you headed?"

"Rome. I'm a film director. We're shooting a big historical epic. Yul Brynner, Yvonne De Carlo and Marlon Brando."

"What a cast! What's it called?"

"*Perils of the Black Flag*," Sam said. "I'm the whatyacawlit. Screen rotter."

"*Perils of the Black Flag*. Wow! So: what's the story?"

Sam lit up. "So. Yool Brinner is this pahrit. Well, *ex*-pahrit. He *was* a pahrit, but he was given wunna them pardons by the Queen of . . ."

"Spain!" I bit my lower lip. "That's Yvonne De Carlo. She's pardoned him on the condition that he works for her, in charge of her . . ."

"Royal fleets! Y'see, this Moorish feller, Count di Veranda—that's Morlin Brindo—he's bin plannin' this attack on the coast o' Spain. Yool Brinner knows all about it, 'cos he was wunce in th' Count's crew."

I jumped in. "So it's brother against brother. They're not really brothers, but they worked together. They were partners in crime. And now they're on the opposite sides of the law."

"That sounds great! What studio's doing this?"

"Warner Brothers."

"M-G-M," Sam said over me.

"Well, it's an independent production. But with this cast, and the setting, we've found ourselves in the middle of a bidding war."

"*Perils of the* . . . hey, everybody!" Herb shouted, and his voice could cut through steel. "We've got a real movie director here!"

Drunken babble turned to a chorus of oohs and aahs. The drunk suburbanites clustered around me. From the corner of my eye, I saw Sam back off into the hallway. He winked at me.

A stone-drunk mom with bad breath asked me all about *Perils of the Black Flag*, and a half hour later I was convinced that it was a great idea for a movie—for someone else to make. Hell, I could write a treatment and sell it to one of the studios, if I knew the right people. I added some other actors to the cast—Elisha Cook Jr., Sidney Greenstreet (who'd been dead for six years) and George Sanders.

I got so lost in invention that I forgot about Sam, or why I was in the booze-soaked home of Herb and Barb Ronson. Sam tapped me on the shoulder and whispered:

Let's git outta here, pordner.

I looked at my watch. "Omigosh! I've got to be on the set at 6 AM! You'll all excuse me. Mrs. De Carlo is *furious* if I'm not there on time."

We passed through a human tunnel of glad-handing and alcohol abuse to the front door. "You call me when you get back," Herb shouted.

My ears rang and my head pounded in the dark cool outside. "Whew." I was a little tipsy. Someone kept refilling my glass while I held court. I sniffled. "So, what happened to you?"

"I was workin'." Sam jingled his pockets. "We done good."

My heart raced. "Good."

"Less git to th' car an I'll show ya."

We got to the car.

FOUR

We did good. Herb and Barb lived large and loose. Exhibit A was a money clip of some precious metal. It held a thick wad of assorted large bills—nothing under a 20. Exhibits B-K: gold baubles and twinkling jewels filled the cup of Sam's hand. "Wow." I started the car and cruised towards a highway.

"There was more. I just skimmed off th' cream."

"Wow."

"Welcome ta the world uh crime, Rick."

"Thank you, Morty."

I turned onto Sunset. Traffic was bustling. The clock on my dashboard read 10:56. "Sam. Have you ever thought about being an actor?"

"Uh nactor? Nah, sir." He thought about it. "But I bet I could do it."

"You're really good at thinking on your feet."

"Trick uh th' trade. You hafta change your plans fast in the real estate game."

I laughed out loud. He mimicked Herb Ronson's voice on that last part.

"I'm serious here. How'd you like to be the lead in my picture?"

"Well . . ." He looked out at the passing traffic. "What's it pay?"

"All you can steal."

A few days later, Artie and I got together with Sam and did a screen test. We filmed him as he strolled around the UCLA campus, by the sea, on Hollywood Boulevard—one reel of black and white and one in color. Sam was a good sport, and while I helped Artie reload the camera, he helped himself to 200 dollars in cash someone left on the front seat of their car.

We screened the test footage in one of the school's workrooms. "He's got something," Artie muttered. "Kinda like that guy in

Breathless."

"Yes. Not as handsome, but he does that squinty-eye thing. He gets your attention."

"I think the camera likes him. Put on the color reel again."

The color footage was filmed mostly near the *Racecar* location. Sam looked like a fish out of water by the seashore. He shrugged his way around the tourists, health-food fanatics, bodybuilders, old people and junkies. In one priceless moment, Sam grooved to a beatnik poet spouting his free-form verse. His delivery had a catchy rhythm, and Sam broke into a million-dollar smile. Even with his crooked teeth, he had a natural charisma that filtered through the camera lens and film stock. It didn't show so much in real life. But the screen made something out of him.

"I think we have our leading man, Artie."

It took four days to convince Sam to say yes. I think he wanted to do it from the start—he figured he could get a few free meals out of me if he strung me along.

Sam wanted to go back to Hody's. I guess he enjoyed the ambiance. The waitresses got to know us well enough to give us the nicknames of "Fric" and "Frac."

I had a standard contract typed up for Sam to sign. Before pen could touch paper, he had two big questions:

what's the film about?
what will I get paid?

I had no clear answer for either. The movie would be about the life of a criminal (or criminals) and would follow them as they did their criminal stuff in a variety of real-life locations. Would they win? Would they lose? Would they die in the last reel? Nobody knew. We would wing it, based on the situations and surroundings.

What—and when—would Sam get paid? This was a low-budget independent production. I was going to sell everything I could to pay for equipment, film stock, transportation, food, lodging and survival. I could scrape up enough to keep our overhead for maybe a month, if we lived on peanut butter and ketchup.

The solution took a while to dawn on me. I woke from a sound sleep. There should have been a light bulb over my head. The idea thrilled me—and seemed so right:

The film's cast would commit real crimes, on camera. The proceeds would finance the production.

To achieve my goals, I'd have to resort to planning and preparation. We'd have to "script" the crimes—plan them out and make sure we could get away with them. There was no way around this part. I would still hope for chance and circumstance to affect the crimes while they were filmed. To make them work—and to keep us from getting caught—the utmost thought and detail would have to go into this part of the film.

The crimes would take up a small part of the movie. We'd spend more time with the criminals between jobs. We'd see them restless, drunk, hung-over, happy, horny, depressed, fretful—in cars, hotel rooms, bus stations . . . wherever we found a good location, and wherever the crimes (and the story) might lead us.

I was excited by this epiphany, but miserable at the idea of all the planning. I supposed it would be good discipline for me. This had to be a marketable motion picture. If it came out the way I felt it would, it would be an artistic triumph. But I had to convince Newton at Crown International that it was good box office. And to be good box office, we had to succeed as criminals.

Flashy jobs, like the bank robberies of *Gun Crazy*, might not be right for this picture. This would be a movie about burglars—about the invasion of private spaces by thieves in search of whatever they saw fit to steal. Maybe there would be a reason why they didn't do bank jobs. That could come out of the actors, as they embodied their roles before the camera.

Sam and I had a lot to discuss. I looked at my wristwatch. It was shy of 5 AM. I was too awake to go back to sleep. I made a pot of coffee and got out my legal pad. Between sips, I wrote down ideas for the characters, their relationship, and the kind of crimes they would commit.

The first idea was check-kiting. We could buy false IDs for the actors, in the names of their characters, and get checks printed up. There were print shops that would run off anything you wanted for the right price.

The downside of this idea: it would be hard to film these transactions, and they're slow on action. Writing bad checks isn't going to keep an audience on the edge of their seats. I'm sure an Alfred Hitchcock could do an effective piece on a man who writes a bad check, in a weak moment, and has his life turned inside-out. It would be a great role for a Henry Fonda or a James Stewart—the affable everyman who weakens under pressure.

I put a *maybe* beside the check-kiting idea.

Robbing a jewelry store? It had been done zillions of times in plays, radio shows, movies, TV and comic books. It wouldn't hold much surprise for the viewer. It could be made suspenseful and involving through whatever might happen during filming. I'd seen some French movies—the old-school, hard-edged crime pictures made after the war—with robbery sequences like this. Maybe it was too well-worn.

Another *maybe*.

Bank robbery was a *maybe* too. That had high stakes—perfect for an exciting story, but perhaps too risky for real-life. We *might* be able to do a perfect bank job. Fate *might* give us all the right breaks. But if one thing went wrong, and we were caught, we'd all face prison sentences and the seizure of our footage.

I drank a pot of coffee and jotted down 14 pages of ideas. By my last cup, I was a jagged mess. I took a shower, shaved and went down to the drugstore to get some food in my gut. I waited until I got some eggs and toast down before I had another cup of coffee. Someone had left one of the morning papers on the stool beside me. I scanned the headlines. Tension, death, uncertainty, cute pictures of puppies. I set the wrinkled paper back down.

Maybe I should do the Otis C. Kenton book as a movie. I could take liberties with the text, as Welles did with *Touch of Evil*.

I ate, paid the check, and walked back to my apartment. I sat down with *Never Odd or Even*. I reread it. Otis C. Kenton had a way with words—terse, sometimes too purple, but his prose passed through you like a blast of warm air.

No. I tossed the book onto the coffee table. It bounced off the edge and landed, spread-eagled, on the carpet. If I did this movie,

I'd take the easy way out. I'd make the same kind of first film all the other darlings of UCLA made. I couldn't go that route.

I thought about other movies I admired—John Cassavetes' *Shadows*, which was filmed on real locations, using people who weren't real actors, and with a lot of the situations improvised. I couldn't make another *Shadows*. It seemed likely that my movie idea could fall into that trap and be dismissed as a watering down of a good idea.

I was on my way down a deep spiral of self-doubt. Good thing Sam showed up.

He just opened the door. He cleared his throat. I jumped, but I snapped out of the horrible zero game in my head. "Hey. Hadn't heard from you. I was wawkin' by . . ."

"You're really good at that."

He smiled. "Year'za practice."

I told him, in a few words, what I was thinking. He listened. Some of it was just babble, but he listened.

"Well . . ." He stopped to think. "You had a good idea, but'cha got too far away from it. Thinkin' too much. That's the worse thing you can do. Gets yuh too far from the real thing. What I do is, I truss my first impression. My first instinct. I size up a place, an' if I'm wrong, I'm wrong, but I'm uzhully right. So: go with y'r gut feelin'. 'At's the best one. All thinkin' does is get in th' way."

"But I'm trying to plan out *how* we can do this picture. I kinda have to . . ."

"*Plannin'*. Now, there's a whole 'nother bawl game." Sam sat on the edge of my coffee table. It was too light to bear his weight, and he almost did a pratfall. He stood up. "I c'd sure use some cawfee."

I made a new pot in the kitchen while he talked. I looked over my shoulder when I could. "Once yew got a good idea, you hafta make shore it's gunna work out. If it don't, you're [a] dead, [b] in jail or [c] . . ." He couldn't think of a [c]. "Les' go t' Hody's. I think better there."

I stopped the brew and grabbed my car keys.

Sam insisted on paying this time. "I had me a good run last night. This time, you get *you* a steak." The kids Hody's loved so much weren't in that evening. It rained, which almost never happens here, and tends to slow the world down. Between bites of his steak, Sam gave me all the free advice I could stomach. "Way I see it, you orta think about this movie like she's a real bank job. 'S gonna be the real thing, right? That's what you been gettin' at, right?"

"Mm hm." I couldn't speak with my mouth full.

"Now, I never done no bank job. You cain't do 'em alone. But I know guys what done 'em and got away with 'em. An' they *always* planned it all out. They went t' the bank, looked it over, got bildin' plans if they could. What I'm sayin' is, they didn't do it on no whim. Ya can't just waltz in an' hole up a gun an' say 'this is a stick-up' like you see on TV."

"Hmm?" I tried to swallow.

"Now, this is your picture. I ain't 'bout to tell yuh how to run yer bidness. But if I wuz you, I'd find a place t' make your pitcher an' put down stakes. Let people know you was in town t' make a pitcher. Give 'em the wrong idea on purpose. Let on y'r makin' another movie 'stead of what's really goin' on. Hell, get the local paper do a story on ya. That's th' best alibi you could have."

"But why would I want to do *that*?"

Sam gave me a blank look. "You make up a story that looks good. An' people see you settin' up the cameras, doin' your film stuff, an' they get all proud about it. It's somethin' special. An' there's no way they would ever think you had nothin' t' do with whatever crime you come up with."

"So: would we stay there after the job? Act like nothing was wrong?"

"S'what *I'd* do." He took in some coffee. "I might have me some pie with ice cream." He flagged a waitress.

They had blackberry pie, so he ordered us each a slice. While we waited, he thought of something. "Aw, shoot. Hadden figured this."
"What?"

"Your movie. Ain't they gunna know you did somethin' 'ginst the law when they see the movie?"

I hadn't given this obvious problem any thought. "You're right. So much for that brilliant plan."

The pie came as our hopes sank. I ate through my angst. I was just about to trash the whole idea and go direct dog food commercials. Then my brain cut through the fog.

"What if there were two crimes?" I swallowed. "One fake one, which we'd film, and a real one, which would happen at the same time, in a different place. *That* would be the one we'd use in the movie, and all people would remember was the staged one. *That* could work. Right?"

Sam nodded. "Lot more plannin' t'make that come off, but yeah, that could work. The ol' subterfuse."

"Subterfuge."

Sam pushed his plate away. Not one crumb or trace of the pie filling remained. "Subterfuse. Now, all you got ta do is fine a place where you c'n git away with all o' this. Not too big, not too small."

I groaned at the thought of all the work ahead of me—ahead of *us*. But if it meant a good, original movie—something that would turn the industry on its ass—I was all for it.

FIVE

By the end of October 1962, I'd found my town—Oregon City, Oregon. Once the state capital, it was eclipsed by Portland, which was 15 miles away. It was a factory town: paper mills bellowed thick smoke and filled the air with toxic crap. Oregon Citians had a chip on their shoulder about their bigger cousin. Half-hearted signs posted through their downtown reminded the visitor that *this* was Oregon's first city. As if anyone cared.

Oregon City's proximity to Portland was ideal. If anything went south, we could split for the bigger city and find someplace to get lost. Until that happened, Portland was handy for renting movie equipment, getting film stock and taking the occasional reasonably clean lungful of air.

Oregon City's downtown was, cinematically speaking, a gift from God. With the silhouettes of the paper mills in the background, its drab stretch of Main Street, lined with miserable shops, felt like a manufactured film set. Any auteur who wanted to assay a dreary meditation on the downfall of small-town America would have fallen to his knees and wept with joy.

Artie and I spent three days in Oregon City. We shot a few reels of black and white 16 and 35mm film. The sky was hazy with smoke, and the wear and tear on the downtown buildings and streets looked magnificent on film. This was where I could get the nervous documentary feeling I wanted.

Artie agreed. "You could win an award just by pointing the camera at a wall here."

Crime was still central to the conceit of *Never Odd or Even*. I felt a pang of reluctance at the idea of committing a for-real felony, but form follows function, and we're all slaves to this rule.

I noticed the savings and loan by accident. I tripped on an uneven wedge in the sidewalk and almost broke my viewfinder. I grabbed a lightpost to stop my fall. Nothing was broken or hurt. I looked up and saw my reflection in the window. My head was framed inside a painted logo. It showed the head of a man, empty but for a smile. Around this head was the business name—*FIRST CITY SAVINGS AND LOAN*—and the slogan: *First in Friendship Since 1937.*

"Excuse me," I said to Artie.

I went inside and looked around. The small S&L was clean, modern and efficient. It had three tellers, two manager-types at desks and a Central Casting small-town security guy. He was 60-something, with big hairy ears, black horn-rimmed glasses and a pleasant, vacant expression. He yawned and grabbed at a fly, lost in post-lunch daydreams.

No one paid me any attention. The three tellers were in mid-transaction. Nervous loan-seekers spoke with the manager-types at each desk. Light, pleasant music played overhead.

Between the teller windows and the bigshot desks was a white marble writing stand, with deposit slips, envelopes and pens attached to brass chains. They had little pocket calendars with the name and address of the business. I got one of those and left.

"Wonder where City Hall is?" I squinted; sunlight seemed stronger through the gauze of the smoke.

"There." Artie pointed to a sign that, in turn, pointed to City Hall. It took the usual amount of BS to find out where a person could get information about properties. I asked for street plans of that whole block. I knew criminals in stories, movies and, perhaps life liked to have diagrams of the buildings where they did their thing. This would be useful to Sam.

On the way out of town, I took photographs of the exterior of First City Savings & Loan. I noticed one side of the building let out into an alleyway near a wide and loud river (the Clackamette, I would soon learn) and a wide and loud arterial road.

We left Oregon City with our test footage and the crinkly rolled-up city plans. We took turns driving back down to LA. Artie had the tendency to fall asleep behind the wheel at night, so we stopped over at whatever fleabag motel we found.

In a Valu-Inn somewhere near the Oregon-California border, we watched a skipping TV in a dingy room and passed a bottle of tequila (not a good idea) back and forth. "Artie, I want you to know that, whatever happens, you're not getting in trouble."

"Why would I?"

"If something goes wrong. And anything could go wrong with this thing. I'll make sure you don't get in trouble."

"Fine. I don't plan to get in trouble."

I sat up. "It's just that *I* could get into trouble. If anyone figures out what we're up to, and we get caught . . ."

"How's about this?" Artie was drunk. He pushed crooked glasses up to his nose. "You don't tell me any more than I hafta know. All I'm doing is shooting this picture—whatever it is—for you. You tell me where to point the camera, I'll point it. Whatever you need. But whatever's going on, I don't know from the script. It's just scenes I get on movie film." He took a swig of tequila. "There *is* gonna be a script. Right?"

"A dummy. Just for show. And for copyright."

Artie wiped his mouth. He looked gray. "So, whenever whatever-it-is happens, you just tell me, 'Artie, we're taking some wild shots. We're going off-script.' How's that?"

"Sure."

"'Scuse me. I have to retch." Artie got rid of the tequila in the bathroom sink. I made my own trip about an hour later.

By year's end, I—we—had things as well planned out as my vision could stand. We had a location, a strong general idea of what I hoped to capture on film, and a location for the on-camera crime that we'd commit to ensure that we had some dynamite box office in-between all the art stuff. Something that Newton would buy.

SIX

Sam scoffed at the floor plans. "This thing don't tell us nothin'. This c'd be 30 years old." I felt dejected—it'd been a lot of time and effort to get that big roll of paper.

The photographs, taken solely for function, made a better impression. "All kyne'za good things *here*." He couldn't tell if the building had a modern alarm system. It was likely that it had some alarm—but the older, the better. "I'd hafta see it fer myself t' be sure."

The building looked unprotected, easy to break into, and hidden by the alleyway and the white noise of the river/traffic. "I'd hafta see 'er fer myself first."

We bought Sam a round-trip bus ticket to Oregon City. Artie turned from the bus as it pulled out. "You know. He might not come back. He might do that job himself."

I shrugged. I couldn't think of anything to say. If Sam bailed on us, there was another criminal and another crime out there somewhere.

While we waited, we got a couple of quick job offers.

One was a dog food commercial. It was storyboarded and just needed a couple of professionals to shoot it. The dog, an exuberant cocker spaniel, shat all over the set. A leather-skinned key grip showed missing teeth in his grin as he confided in me: "Sometimes y' just wanna *kick* those little bastards."

The work paid okay, and I didn't find it horrible. There was no room for imagination—just point the camera at the big bag of dog food, get a couple of good shots of the dog gobbling it down (like Sam and his steak) and try not to step in the dog crap. I was the envy of some of my film-school comrades for getting the professional work. Poor saps—they'd have sold their souls to do this for life.

We were doing a reshoot on a spot for Alpha-Bits cereal when I got word from Sam. He sent a postcard from Oregon City:

ITS A SURE FIRE BETT. UNLESS I AM "MISSING"
SOMETHING A KID COULD DO IT. SEE YOU SOON.

The kid on the Alpha-Bits spot had a hard time with the newer,
stupider tagline an ad agency had dreamed up—the reason for
this reshoot. His lisp, which was the reason he was hired, murdered
the tagline. A nervous Nell from the agency tried not to have a fit,
but he made the kid keep flubbing the line.

After two hours of hell for the kid, someone decided to get a
voice artist to overdub the tagline. We'd gone into overtime, and
the union rep began to bark. We had the footage, and I was more
interested in the details of my sure-fire bett.

Sam woke me out of a sound sleep. It was raining. "Come git me,
Chorlie."

"Where are you?" I stepped into my pants as he told me. I couldn't
find a raincoat or umbrella. I got soaked going from the lobby to
my car. It wasn't cold, but I hated to get my leather upholstery
wet. I hoped to have this car for another five years.

Sam huddled under an awning outside the bus station. I honked;
it made him jump. He dashed through the rain. I'd forgotten to
unlock the passenger door. He was soaked by the time he flopped
onto the seat.

"Where you want to go?"

Sam shrugged. "Where *you* goin'?"

I sighed. "Home. Back to sleep."

Sam looked at his lap. "Well. I ain't 'zactly got anyplace t' go . . ."

I knew a long story was coming and cut it off. "You can sleep on
my couch. For tonight."

"Hey, thanks, Chorlie." He smiled. "An' wait 'til y'hear about this
place . . ."

"Let's run over it in the morning. I'm too tired to think."

"Sorry I woke you up."

"Don't worry about it."

We rode in silence. I focused on staying conscious. Sam's exhales
had a wheezy sound—probably from that dirty air in Oregon City.

We made one last dash through the rain. I unlocked my door and pointed at the couch. I may have mumbled "good night" on my way to bed.

Sam snored and talked in his sleep. Both woke me up and made me determined not to share a sleeping space with him again. He repeated a cryptic phrase in his sleep: "Get *off* me, hungry!" I had no idea what this meant, and I wasn't about to ask.

And here's where *Summer and Sandy* comes in. Without it, *Never Odd or Even* wouldn't exist. It was a sincere, derivative, teen drama penned by an asexual, soft-spoken kid from Virginia named Barrett Broadford.

Barrett was the square in my social circle. We studied together at UCLA—me in directing, he in screenwriting. Devoted to film as I, he longed for mainstream acceptance. His personality and writing had that "aw, shucks," shoe-tips-gently-kicking-at-the-sand quality that brought us safe, respectable Oscar-winning material. His favorite film was *The Member of the Wedding*, and his ambition was to make movies of that ilk.

Nothing wrong with that idea. I've never liked such fare, but the majority of moviegoers love such maudlin, touching, kissy-feely kind of drama, and good for them. It keeps the Academy Awards nominators on their toes and gives Hollywood something to point to with pride when its critics complain about the LCD of American cinema.

Okay—*Summer and Sandy*. It was Barrett's thesis screenplay, and tailor-made for a novice director. One of those pictures that, like the dog food commercials I'd shot, only required the filmmaker to show up, rehearse the actors and point the camera in the right direction. The script was the show, and it offered any young male and female newcomers a strong debut role.

I'd coached Barrett through its many drafts, and I felt that he had the right touch of sensitivity—and dynamite subject matter— to make *Summer and Sandy* a hot property.

It's set in an unnamed town in the Deep South. Sandy, 17, is "special." He is sensitive, artistic and moody. It's suggested—never said out loud—that he is mentally challenged. Today, we'd call

Sandy autistic.

Lisa, also 17, is in love with Sandy. A child at heart, Sandy plays with Lisa's love like the oil paints he squeezes onto his palette.

He won't make love to her, but he will paint her. And with his paints and brush, he makes love to her through incisive and masterful portraits. As he paints, he and Lisa become closer. Or so she thinks. Unknown to her is the news that Sandy has been accepted to an art college in New York City. As soon as summer is over, he'll pack up his Rorschach tests and linseed oil and leave Hicksburg behind.

Lisa discovers this on the eve of his departure. Her heartbroken tears change something in Sandy, and he becomes a man (in a scene I co-wrote, uncredited; Barrett had no clear idea how the love-making process worked). At script's close, Lisa joins Sandy on the bus to Manhattan. The stars are in their eyes and a bright future shines as the Greyhound rumbles down a hillbilly highway at dawn. Fade to black.

An obvious hit. The kind of picture they love to run to death on Turner Classic Movies. But Barrett was so sensitive, so shy, that he couldn't bring himself to hire an agent, or otherwise maneuver to get his script on the desk of any studio exec.

The idea came from a comment of Sam's—that we would pretend to shoot a second movie while making our real project. I was taking a dump when the memory of *Summer and Sandy* came back to me. I called Barrett and asked him to meet me for lunch.

"No kidding?" Barrett's sensitive eyes were as wide as thoughtful, understanding saucers. "Oh, Charles! This is a dream come *true* for me!" He sipped on his cherry coke.

"I've been casting around for something really solid for my first feature." I exhaled smoke away from pure, clean Barrett. "I read a stack of scripts yea-high" (I made a foot-wide gap between my hands) "and nothing seemed right. And then I remembered yours."

I discussed my ideas: that I wanted to shoot it with two unknowns, film it on location out of the state, and make it in a naturalistic style better than the "realistic" dramas the studios churned out by the carload for Oscar bait. Mine would be different.

Mine would be sincere—a reflection of the thoughtful and tender writing of Barrett Broadford.

"You'll want me there on the set." His voice was breathless, as if there was another answer.

I was ready to make up any excuse why he shouldn't be there. Then it dawned on me. He would be the perfect alibi. An up-and-coming "important" screenwriter, taking part in the production of his debut script, in a powerful new picture to never be released anywhere.

"Of course." I sipped my martini. "I wouldn't have it any other way."

On a contingency handshake, I empowered one gentle, under-experienced writer to the core of his dreamy soul and gave *Never Odd or Even* its perfect backstory.

Now we're caught up. So back to Sam. He snored and muttered until 10 AM, when I opened the living room drapes with a snap and let all the sunshine of Southern California onto his face. He stirred, grunted and held his hands over his eyes. "Whut th' *fuck*, man?"

"Time's a-wastin'. Want some coffee?" Sam sat up, disheveled in his traveling clothes, and accepted a cup without comment. He waved me away. "Gotta gimme a minute."

I gave him an hour. Then I laid the *Summer and Sandy* business on him. I expected him to put up a fight, but he thought it was brilliant. "Yeah! What-you call. One of them Trojan horse deals. Say one thing, do another. That's smort, Chorlie."

And now the big boom. "And you're going to play the part of Sandy. You're perfect for it."

"Whut?" Sam tried to back into the couch. He didn't get far. "I ain't uh *actur*! I won't *do* it!"

I explained to him that he *would* do it and put his heart and soul into it. Because we were going to make *Summer and Sandy*; the plan wouldn't work without it.

After three more cups of coffee, Sam dug his notes from his pockets. He'd written them in pencil on the inside of matchbooks, in the columns of newspapers, on anything that he could stash away in a hurry.

Only he could decipher his own handwriting. A couple of times, he'd show me a word and ask, "What's *this* say?" I had no answer.

The upshot of all his notes and diagrams: First City Savings & Loan was a pushover—a piece of cake. "Even *you* c'd do this job. It'zat *easy*."

He'd picked the lock on the alley-side door with a standard burglar's pocket tool. No alarms went off. He walked around inside the dark layout, unknown and unseen. "The doorway's all ruint from the wet weather. Half the time I betcha c'd just push hard on th' door an she'd pop open."

Before Sam could suggest another meal at Hody's, I made some scrambled eggs and bacon and put another pot of coffee on. We ate, and then I called Artie. I think I woke him, but he agreed to come over for a conference. I hadn't sprung *Summer and Sandy* on him, either. Now was the time.

"Wow," Artie said, at least eight times. He knew Barrett and had heard about *Summer and Sandy*. "Do you have an option on the script?"

"A verbal one. Barrett's really thrilled."

"You want to get that in writing. When do we start?" I wanted to get to Sam's discoveries about First City Savings & Loan, but Artie wouldn't budge. He said *Sandy* was "the best idea you've ever had," "a sure-fire thing" and "I can't wait to get started."

After an hour of Artie's badgering, I called Barrett. He came over, breathless, with a copy of the *Summer and Sandy* screenplay. Artie acted as pushy as a producer. He drafted up a contract that he wanted the three of us to sign. "My uncle's a notary public. I can get him to witness it." He volunteered to type up the contract and left my place rabid with enthusiasm. Sam and I hadn't a moment to say boo about *Never Odd or Even* or Oregon City.

Sam was asleep on my unmade bed, snoring and mumbling. With Artie gone, I nudged him awake. He gathered himself together and stumbled into the living room. One tail of his shirt stuck out from his trousers. He needed a shave and his hair was a black haystack.

"*This* is our Sandy." I gestured to Sam. Barrett's eyes widened. He looked worried—first at me, then at the universe.

"I ain't no actur," Sam muttered. He tried to straighten his hair with his fingertips without success. Then he flopped down on the couch.

"That's why you're *perfect* for the role. You're a real *person*—not some phony Warren Beatty type." I handed the screenplay to Sam. He accepted it with reluctance. He didn't open it. "I'd like for you to read for the part. I'll read Lisa's lines."

"Aw, shit." Sam slumped deeper into the couch, like that would protect him from what I asked him to do.

"Humor me. Read one page with me. Just so Barrett can hear." Sam grunted and crossed his arms. "If Barrett here doesn't like your reading, we'll forget all about it. Okay?"

Sam grunted louder. He sat up a little.

I found a good scene early in the script. This establishes the relationship of Sandy and Lisa—she's adoring and fawning; he's distracted and indifferent. It's during her first portrait sitting, in the attic studio in Sandy's house.

This scene became one of the central pieces in the movie, for better or worse:

INT. ATTIC – LATE AFTERNOON

LISA, dressed in a simple skirt and top, sits self-consciously atop a wooden stool. She positions herself with great care, looking up to see if Sandy takes notice of her.

SANDY mixes paint colors on his wooden palette. He glances up at Lisa now and then, but his attention is fixed to his preparation for the painting.

LISA: You know, I've never had my portrait painted before. (pauses) I don't believe I've even been photographed. Can you believe that? (stops to think) Oh, no. That's not right. Out at my grandmother's—she took some pictures of me last summer. (looks at Sandy) Didn't mother show them to you?

Sandy shrugs, one paintbrush in his teeth. He goes back to his mixing.

LISA: They were such nice pictures. I was sitting on the old porch swing—under the blooming wisteria. That smell was in the air—just like perfume. A gentle perfume. And then it started to rain.

SANDY: Rain?

LISA: You know—one of those gentle spring rains. The ones where it feels like the raindrops are kissing the ground. Not battering it to death like those summer downpours. Those are so . . . so . . . so brutal. Don't you agree? (pause) All that rain in the sky. Makes the world seem so . . . so hopeless.

Sandy looks up. He stands up and approaches Lisa.

SANDY: I always liked the rain. It makes you think. You know? Makes you stop and think.

LISA (brightly): How shall I sit?

SANDY: Just sit. Like you always sit. Don't make it fancy.

LISA: As you like. But it always seems that the people in paintings aren't just . . . sitting. They're . . . they're saying something with their bodies. (pauses; nervously) What do I say to you when I'm sitting? What am I saying to you?

SANDY: You want the honest truth?

Lisa nods.

SANDY: You're saying all this stuff about . . . photographs and grandmothers and . . . and the rain. And it's confusing me. It's confusing me, Lisa. I wish I could tell you it meant something big. Anything important. But it's just a lot of hot words—spilling out all over me. (pauses) I can't take all these words . . . all this talk. That's why I do what I do. Here. Where it's quiet. In my attic.

Sandy stands up and looks out an attic window. Lisa stands behind him, obviously hurt by his words.

LISA: I didn't mean to—to . . . annoy you. Sandy.

SANDY: You don't annoy me. Words. They annoy me. Everyone so in love with the sound of their words. Their voices. All jabbering. Tick, tick, tick. Like some demented clock. On and on and on . . .

Sandy turns to Lisa, near tears.

SANDY: I—I'm no good with words. I make pictures. I want to make your picture. Not your words. 'Cos there's too many words. And not enough pictures.

Sandy gently sits Lisa down on the stool. He props her head up and smiles.

SANDY: So: if you'll just sit here and be yourself—without words— I'm going to paint you. Without words.

LISA: (after a long pause; almost as a whisper) Without words.

Sandy smiles and puts an index finger to his lips. As he begins to sketch Lisa's figure in charcoal on the canvas, rain patters on the attic ceiling. Sandy and Lisa make eye contact. Lisa almost says something but keeps her promise. She smiles as the drum of the rain deepens . . .

Sam surprised himself. He got into the character. For a cold reading, he did fine. It convinced Barrett that my choice of Sam was solid. And I think it convinced Sam that he was indeed an actur. "I could see that scene in black and white." Barrett stood up, excited. "Just like it was on film. Terrific!"

"I don't really see myself as Lisa," I joked. "I guess we need to find a Lisa."

"And an Aunt Myra," Barrett said with gravity. "But a *Lisa* is most important. Now that we have our Sandy. *If*," he said to Sam, "you'll agree to do it."

"Well . . ." Sam shrugged like he didn't have anything better to do. "I hope I don't let nobody down . . ." I put on a new pot of coffee.

SEVEN

Artie got all of us together in his uncle's office. His uncle did something with investments. He was bald as an egg. His uncle's secretary typed the contract that bound Barrett Broadford, Charles Jerome and *Summer and Sandy* for the purposes of the making of a motion picture, to be independently produced by Charles Jerome and Arthur Sellon.

Later that week, I had meetings at Columbia and Universal, which were a waste of my time and theirs. United Artists agreed to finance the production, with the understanding that this would be a low-budget A picture. Since it had no box-office stars, it was technically a risk for them. But they knew that Barrett's screenplay was Oscar bait. If it were filmed right, in black and white and using found locations—not studio sets—it would be one of their big pictures of 1963.

Now I *had* to make *Summer and Sandy*. I'd signed documents stating that I would. I knew I could make a good picture—by commercial standards—from Barrett's sincere script. It would be the biggest dog food commercial I'd ever done.

My days split between time with Sam, where I was exposed to a world unknown to me, and sessions with Barrett, which cloyed in their unending earnestness. I began to prefer Sam's company, and as I learned more about his life, I got a clearer image of his character in *Never Odd or Even*.

Sam would be himself—a low-key person with a history of violence. Many of Sam's stories went something like this: "So I'm just sittin' on the stoop watchin' the wurl' go by an I realize I'm outta smokes. Now I quit them things in jail—prolly the one smort thing I done in my life. But then, y'see, I was still smokin'.

"So this black dude goes struttin' by. Big guy, well-dressed, looked like he knew what was goin' on. So I thawt: there ain't no horm in askin'. 'Hey, man, you got a smoke?'

"Maybe I shoulda said pretty please. 'Cos this guy turned on me an' he was mad! 'What th' fuck did you say t' me?' I mean, this guy is *angry*! An' here I'm just a kid, not even 17, just killin' time on the street.

"So, he pulls me up by th' collars of my coat, an' we're face t' face. I can smell his breath. He'd had a few. He don't take his eyes offa mine. 'What th' *fuck* did you *just say* to *me*?' I try to talk but my throat is dead. I swaller an smile, tryin t' explain but the words won't come out, but then again I can't say nothin', so he thinks I'm comin' on to him or somethin'. An *WHAM!* He pops me one in the nose. I see white an' I taste blood. He drops me an *BAM!* I feel th' toe of his shoe hit my stomach. I'm doubled over, seein' everything like a blur. An' one word comes outta me. An' yew know what that word was?"

I hadn't the slightest idea. I shrugged.

"*Jerry!* Cos, see, that was my uncle Jerry. He was in the Marines durin' the wore, an' he was one bad sumbitch. He's how come I come to California. So this spade is lettin' me have it, an I'm seein' my life goin' before my eyes. An' it ain't a good one. But two sekkins after I called for him, Jerry's there. An *BAM!* he cold-cocks that spade right out to the street.

"Before he could get off the ground, Jerry give him reason to lose a couple teeth. Me, I'm tryin' to get on my feet an' up the stairs. I felt like that spade kicked a hole in my gut. It burns like fire. But I get ahold of the banister and get up.

"Meanwhiles, Jerry has this black guy beggin' him t' stop. Somebody called the cops, an' we heard sirens. The black guy just disappears. Jerry ain' got a scratch on 'im. Just some blood on his shirt. We just go back inside. Close the door.

"'What the fuck was all *that* about?' Jerry looks daggers at me. I tole him all I ast was could I bum a smoke. Jerry calls me all kinda names and says how stupid can you get, try'na ask a black guy for anything. So, Uncle Jerry showed me how t' use my dukes—" Sam made a pair of fists—"an' that waddn't all he showed me."

Jerry was Sam's conduit into a life of crime. He showed Sam the ropes in the art of burglary, robbery and other felonies. Sam was a good student. He learned that the lowest profile suited his type the best. "Jerry was always a big mouth. Could'n' quit braggin' about where he'd been, what he'd done. He tawked hisself into prison. He's still there. Me, I never tole anyone nothin'." He stopped to sip his cold coffee. "'Cept you. You're the first, Chorlie."

"You've never been caught?"

"Nope." Sam smiled. "Come close more 'n once. Been in jail once. Had nothin' t' do with what I do. I just served my time an' shut my mouth. That's all I got to say about that. I seen 'em come, I seen 'em go. But I keep myself quiet. That's the secret."

"You ever had a real job?"

"Couple. Tole you 'bout the delivery bidness. Last year, I worked in a warehouse. That was a good job 'til they canned my ass. You could boost stuff—make sumpin' onna side. Like, they ain't gonna miss a color TV here an' there. That kinda bidness."

If I wrote a script about Sam, he'd have been too much to believe. But having Sam be *himself* in a movie—without any expectations— could be riveting. I hoped that his role in *Summer and Sandy* wouldn't spoil that natural quality.

Artie and I blocked out *Sandy*, and took a trip to Oregon City, on UA's dime, to scout locations. We had a checklist of settings: a large house with a porch and an attic; a Main Street of storefronts; a library; a church; various outdoor spots.

We found them all, plus some good places that we'd work into the movie as we shot. Artie also served as art director, and he said we didn't need to touch a thing—except to put new signs on some of the shops.

We talked a couple of small businesses into letting us paint fictional names on their windows for the duration of shooting. They'd be able to brag that their shoe repair shop or diner was in a real honest-to-God Hollywood picture. The stipend we paid them was for good will's sake. We wanted the locals on our side.

Artie brought up *Never Odd or Even.* "You really going to make this thing?"

"Yes. We'll shoot that at night. Do it in hotel rooms, bowling alleys—wherever we can set up a camera. It'll be a hard schedule, but we'll come out of it with two pictures. One will be good and the other . . ." I lost my train of thought.

"It's just . . . you got a career here. You make this *Sandy*, and you'll be in. Then you'll be able to make some great movies. I don't want to see you go to prison, on account of some crazy idea . . ."

"It isn't crazy. I know what I'm doing." I hadn't laid any of Sam's stories on Artie yet. I respected Sam's desire for a low profile. I knew that Sam could navigate us through his world, and if that world could be caught on movie film, and its sounds sucked onto magnetic tape, *Summer and Sandy* would come off looking quaint in comparison.

People like quaint. I know that. But I was past quaint. Quaint played it safe, went for the easy outs; made gentle people feel good about themselves. Quaint wasn't what made the films that I loved.

Hurrah for the gentle people. I wasn't one of them. Not anymore.

On the night before we left Oregon City, I coaxed Artie into the rain. We drove to First City Savings and Loan. I wanted to try out a trick Sam showed me.

With an ice pick and a paper clip, hidden in the dark of the alley, I easily opened the side door to the place. I walked inside the savings and loan. Dark and echoey inside, the building was empty. "Come on," I hissed to Artie. "It won't kill you."

We explored the place for 10 minutes. The manager's office door wasn't locked. I drew a KILROY WAS HERE on the last page of his desk blotter. Artie walked back from the cashier area with a roll of nickels. "You think they'll miss these?" He laughed.

"Put that back. We don't want them to know anyone's been in here."

Artie's joy deflated and he shuffled back to the teller's counter. "So. What now?"

"Nothing. Just wanted you to see how easy this is."

"How the hell am I gonna *light* this place?" Some lights were on, but it was dim inside. Klieg lights would stand out in the nighttime, even with the blinds drawn. Someone would see our shadows. We'd have to figure out a way to add enough light to film, and to work without attracting attention.

"We'll figure it out. C'mon." I opened the door to the alley. Looked both ways, then looked again. It was quiet. The rain drummed down, and cars whished through the wet in the night. Once Artie was out, I pulled the door until I heard the lock click. So: it *did* lock. We walked toward the street. Artie sniffled; the climate here was hell on his sinuses.

The police car surprised us as we came out on the sidewalk. The cops didn't notice us. I hissed at Artie. He saw what I saw and ducked behind me. We walked past the cops. The one in the passenger's seat glanced up at me. I nodded and smiled. He nodded and smiled back.

The light changed and traffic moved. Artie kept his nose to the ground at his feet. He stood between two storefronts. "'Scuse me. I have to retch."

He retched.

EIGHT

If you've ever had to do a hard job that went against everything you enjoyed, you can relate to how I felt during pre-production on *Summer and Sandy*. Storyboards. Rehearsals. Budget meetings. Casting calls. All of it the things that normal film-makers do as a matter of course. It was all dog food to me.

We found our Lisa in a play at UCLA that somebody dragged me to see. Charlotte Magill had the role of Fenny in an Americanized revival of *Dear Octopus*, a British play from the 1930s. I liked the play's lack of plot—the selling point of the friend who insisted I see it—but Charlotte Magill won me over.

She was 22, but she looked like a high-school senior. She had that quiet, focused *something* that I could see in the character of Lisa. And she interacted well with older actors, so she would be fine with our Aunt Myra. We got Irene Ryan for that role—Granny from *The Beverly Hillbillies*, right before she got typecast in that part.

I was a pro. I didn't approach Charlotte after the performance. I went through the chain of command. A publicist at UA knew her major professor at UCLA. A meeting was arranged, and I gave her the pitch for the movie. She left with a copy of the screenplay and assured me she'd read it.

Two days later, her person called my person to tell me that she'd read *Summer and Sandy* and loved it. Her person asked my person if she could have my phone number. She also wanted to meet her co-star—if his people would agree.

I was Sam's people, but I didn't say so. I did say yes to the phone number exchange. It was like an arranged marriage. Casual protocol, but strictly adhered to by all parties.

Charlotte and I met in a quiet cafe in Westwood. She brought the script with her. It was dog-eared and showed other signs of rough handling. I spotted her before she saw me. I stood up to greet her. "Miss Magill."

"Charlotte. *Please*."

"Charlotte. Good to see you."

"Oh, Mister *Jerome*!" She slid into the booth. The script fell from her hands, still bent into a U shape as it fanned out on the tabletop.

"Charlie. *Please*."

"I've . . . I've *got* to play Lisa. It's like . . . like the writer was looking over my shoulder. Just writing down my thoughts. I've never come across a character that was so . . . just . . . *me*."

She knew Barrett through other UCLA friends, but hadn't gotten that he was a screenwriter. "*He* wrote *this*? I thought he was . . . you know . . . *queer*." She laughed and seemed embarrassed that she'd spoken the word.

I thought Barrett might be light in the loafers too, but I'd never pressed the point. Who cares? You are who you are. That's it.

The next obstacle: putting Lisa and Sam together. Would they click? *Could* they click? Sam didn't eat well, didn't sleep well, didn't bathe on a reliable basis. He needed to be domesticated.

I had to get him spruced up for the meeting. If Charlotte didn't like Sam, we were SOL. We got together to eat (yes, at Hody's) one afternoon and I brought up the topic.

"Ain't nothin' wrong with *me*." Sam stirred his mashed potatoes and gravy into beige putty on his plate.

"All you need is a little polish. Just comb your hair. Shave. Get some better clothes. You gotta make a good first impression. This is like a date. She's gotta like you. And vice versa."

Sam sneered at his coffee. Then he took a sip. "Z'all porta the plan. Right?"

"Right."

"Then we gotta do it." He finished his coffee. A drop lingered on his chin. "But we gonna do 'er *my* way."

Sam shoplifted a sharp new wardrobe, two or three items at a time. He showed me his go-to trick for getting new shoes. We drove to a shopping center in Westwood. Before he got out of the car, he took off his shoes. He had on black socks. He saw my *what the hell?!* look. "Z'all porta the roo-teen. C'mawn." He guided me towards a posh shoe shop. A bell tinkled as he opened the door. A guy who looked like I hoped Sam would look—Ivy League sharp—greeted us and asked how he could help.

"Muh buddy here's gittin' hitched. Needs s'm nice dress shoes." I caught the gist in time and looked nervous. I tried to smile like a guy who's about to wreck his life. I nodded and tugged at my shirt collar.

While the clerk showed me seven pairs of shoes, and I pretended to settle for an 80-dollar job, Sam chose some cordovan penny loafers. Just slipped them on, tucked the box under a chair, and walked over to us. "Made up y'r mind, Chet?"

"You know, I think this pair will do. But I need to run this past my tailor. Can you please put these on hold for me? And can I have your business card?"

Chet Nixon never did come back for those shoes. I don't think he got married. But Sam got a beautiful pair of loafers, just right for the impression I hoped to make. Until someone discovered that empty box under the chair, no one would be the wiser.

The Sams of the world are the reason you can't shoplift anymore. They're why socks have those theft-proof plastic doodads that cashiers struggle to scan and remove. The only item of clothing he couldn't lift was a sports coat, and I paid for that—something I could claim on my income tax, so I saved the receipt.

I didn't feel like I was anyone to tell Sam how to live his life. But I made some strong suggestions. With snorts of protest and laughter, Sam listened to my Dating Dos & Don'ts. He agreed to try not to swear in front of Charlotte, not to steal anything (ashtray, sugar container, menu) and to be polite.

We worked up a good back story, so she'd buy him as an up-and-coming young actor. In those beautiful days before search engines or smartphones existed, one could lie and, within reason, expect to get away with it. Charlotte grew up in Southern California, so all her connection to the world of drama was Los Angeles-based.

I decided Sam was from Baltimore, based on his accent. We invented a drama professor named Dexter Stein, and had him at Towson University ("good old TU"). There, Sam had appeared in some Shakespeare, Ibsen and O'Neill (his Long in a student production of *The Hairy Ape* got him strong notices).

Sam drove out to LA from Baltimore on a lark, and his car (a Pontiac Bonneville convertible) was totaled in Burbank. Thus, Sam decided to make lemonade, and had been making inquiries at the studios. United Artists discovered him (not a total lie) and he was a shoo-in for the role of Sandy.

It bothered Sam to have to go over this stuff, just as it bugged him to get his hair cut or bathe every day. But by the day of the meeting, he was in good working order. It looked like this short con would work.

"Not to make you nervous." I found a spot in front of the cafe and stole it from another driver. "But this has to go right. You impress Miss Magill, and we're in like Flynn."

Sam checked his hair in the rearview mirror. He cleaned up well. His posture still needed work, but slouching was the in thing.

"I think you'll like Miss Magill." I saw her in one of the booths and waved. She was lost in thought but snapped out of it and smiled. "Here we go," I whispered. I put my hand on Sam's shoulder and guided him towards destiny.

Charlotte stood up. She and I exchanged a brief hug (since we'd met before) and I introduced Sam. "Ma'am." He smiled with a genuine kindness. They shook hands. Charlotte and I sat on one side of the booth. Sam slid into the other seat, careful not to crease his smart Ivy League sports blazer. He wore a dark blue silk shirt with no tie, gray-green slacks that went well with his ochre blazer, dark blue socks and those cordovan loafers, which kind of didn't go with the other colors, but who looks at a man's shoes? Not shoe store clerks!

Charlotte and Sam got to know one another. They told their back stories. Charlotte's sounded as contrived as his. She was a suburban girl who saw a production of *Hamlet* at age 8 and had wanted to be an actress ever since.

She'd worked at it. From high school plays to community theater to bit parts in TV shows and movies, she kept working on her art, whether it was a nice role in a respected play or Second Onlooker in an *Alfred Hitchcock Presents* show.

The subject turned to *Summer and Sandy.* "I've read the screen play seven times now. You know how it is. You just have to live inside it. Get to know it backwards and sideways. And forwards."

"I'm workin' on my lines too, Miss Magill."

"Charlotte. *Please.*"

"Shorelot. Ma'am. I think it's a good show." He pointed to the curlicued script on the table. "Lotta drama there."

Charlotte looked at the script and smiled. Light played in her eyes. "I have a mad idea! Why don't you and I read a scene? Right now?"

I heard Sam swallow. "I . . . I *guess* we could . . ."

"Do you have a favorite scene . . . Sam?"

Sam looked at me. "Well, Shorelot, I . . . I *do.*" He picked the scene we'd read in front of the author. If it worked for Barrett Broadford, what the hell?

"I'll read the stage directions. Screen directions." I shrugged. "Whatever ya call 'em." I got up and motioned for Sam to take my place. "I'll be the director."

"This is *wonderful!*" I think Charlotte clapped her hands with glee.

"INT. ATTIC – LATE AFTERNOON," I read. "LISA, dressed in a simple skirt and top, sits self-consciously atop a wooden stool. She positions herself with great care, looking up to see if Sandy takes notice of her . . ."

Charlotte and Sam read together like old pros. I was surprised. They had . . . *chemistry.* Though they read someone else's contrived words off a mimeographed page, they brought life to their dialogue, and gave me the sense that this was going to work. We were going to pull this off.

Sam got nervous and stammered. It was perfect for the moment when Sandy starts on his rant about people talking: "Tick tick tick . . ." Did Sam realize he could act?

Of course, he did. To be a good criminal, you have to be a good actor, a good liar and you have to put on a convincing front of the person (or persons) that you're not. He could play a character. That's what he did all day. Even with me.

Charlotte Magill and Sam Mellinger sparked as actors as they brought that precious little scene to life. I could tell Charlotte was sold on Sam. And the way Sam smiled sheepishly—totally against his invented devil-may-care collegiate backstory—told me he liked this lie. He could get accustomed to it.

I reported back to Artie and Barrett, and to my people at United Artists. Their people talked to Charlotte Magill's people, who talked to me (Sam's people) and contracts were drafted, addended and signed with a handshake.

Variety announced that "Charles Jerome, UCLA wonder boy of *Racecar* renown, has inked a pact with United Artists to direct the original screen story *Summer with Sandy* [sic] as an indie prod. Newcomers Charlotte Magill and Sam Mellinger will star. Pic is to be shot on authentic locations in Oregon. Script by recent UCLA grad Barry [sic] Broadfort [sic] is a hot property, with other studios asking about the young scribe's future services. Shooting is to begin July 1st . . ."

And we were off to the races. I was excited about the whole thing. Though I knew I'd get impatient with the normal process of making a feature film—knowing what was going to happen and going through the motions of making it happen over and over, if necessary—the challenge of making a second movie, unknown to United Artists or anyone but Artie and Sam, was thrilling to me.

What that movie would be, and what *shape* it might take, was unknown to anyone too. All I had was a germ of an idea. I hated to think too much on it. I wanted complete honesty, spontaneity, improvisation—real life. That's all I had to go on with *Never Odd or Even.*

Every nuance of *Summer and Sandy* was spelled out in its screenplay, in the locations we'd claimed, the camera moves Artie and I sketched out on typing paper, like panels of a comic strip. We taped those crude sketches on the wall of Artie's rec room. Close-ups, two-shots, medium shots, pans across landscapes. Every camera movement, every object in the film frame planned, deliberate, there on purpose.

Artie thrived on this structure and organization. It felt to me like he put twice what was needed into *Summer and Sandy*. He called it *ducks in a row*. "We got our ducks in a row, Charlie. *Look* at that." Prop lists, phone numbers, addresses, camera lens settings, exposure charts, wardrobe, and papers, papers, papers, contracts, agreements, checklists, shot lists, schedules, transportation arrangements . . . a thousand waterfowl in a long, complex row.

Without the promise of freedom *Never Odd or Even* held for me, I couldn't have lived with myself. Or with how the whole thing played out. And we'll get into every gruesome detail of that. If that's the only reason you're reading this, shame on you.

NINE

With *Sandy* a sure thing, I sat Artie down and had The Talk. "I'm making two movies. One has a script, and a cast. The other doesn't."

"Doesn't what?"

I sighed. "You know what I *mean*. The thing is, *I'm* gonna make two movies while we're in Oregon. How about you?"

Artie stirred his coffee in silence.

"I'm . . . I'm giving you a chance to back out." I grabbed Artie's hand to stop his stirring and get his attention. "You can make *Summer and Sandy* with me. That's what I want. I couldn't make it without you."

"Thank you." Artie tasted his coffee. It was too sweet.

"But if you don't want to trouble yourself with the other movie, I don't blame you. No hard feelings is what I mean. You don't really seem to think it's a good idea. It wouldn't—"

Artie frowned. "Fine. Let's *make* the damned thing. But if *you* fall on your face with it, that's *your* red wagon. The important thing—" he signaled the waitress for a refill—"the important thing is that we make this *Summer and Sandy*, and that we get a great picture from it. This one can *make* us, Charlie. It's got a good script, a good cast . . ."

"I'm a professional. I'm going to do my best. But I'm not gonna sign on for a lifetime of pictures like this. I'll be a good boy. I'll play by the rules. They'll think they've got me where they want me. And then I'll let 'em have it with *Never Odd or Even*. Then they won't know *what* to make of me."

"Fine. If you can have your cake and eat it too, more power to you. Honey, here." Artie already acted and sounded like his father. The embarrassed (and harassed) waitress refilled our cups with a hard glare. Then Artie poured about a third of the sugar container into his coffee. He stirred, stirred, stirred. Took a sip; winced. "Something off about this coffee tonight." He cleared his throat without success. "So . . . what," he croaked, "*is* this picture gonna be about, anyway?"

"Well . . . it's about what it's like to be a criminal. What your life is like when you wake up, and you're on the wrong side of the law. You're probably living in some dump, or holed up in a hotel with bedbugs in the mattress and mold on the walls. You don't sleep well, you don't eat well. But you only know this life. You couldn't put it behind you and become an accountant. Your life is about taking what doesn't belong to you. That's your job.

"Maybe you have *some* personal ethics. Maybe you stop short at killing people to get what you want. Maybe you only steal from people who are too rich to miss the loss. Maybe you have a personal vendetta that you have to take care of. But you're devoted to your work. You take it seriously.

"When you're in some crummy hotel on a highway, and you watch an old gangster flick on TV, you laugh because the movies always get it wrong. They try to glamorize the life of a criminal. And at the same time, they criticize the criminal and say that he's a bad person. And who's to say that he is? Morally, he comes from a different place than what we've been told is good. But maybe he's seen 'good' people do worse things to others than *he's* ever done. Maybe he's seen poor people trampled on, evicted from their homes, getting everything they owned taken away from them . . ."

"You sound like Tom Joad." Artie smiled. "But you got something there. I never saw a picture that talked about crime from that angle. From the driver's seat."

"That's *it*! That's *exactly* what I want to do. To show that it's just another career some people fall into. Some people get out at the right time. They cut and run, and go on to live a 'normal' life, say hi to the mailman, get married, join the PTA. But they'll always carry that past life with them. And they'll always be tempted by the idea to try it again. And maybe they do. Maybe they stick up a dry cleaner in another town, just to show themselves that they still have it.

"I'm not saying crime is good or bad. I'd just like to make a movie that showed it as it *is*—not as some Hollywood bore's idea of what it *might* be."

Artie mock-applauded. "I get where you're comin' from, brother. Good stuff." He drank his coffee. "So, are the kids gonna be in it?"

"*Sam* is . . ." I realized I hadn't thought about how Charlotte Magill would/wouldn't fit into *Never Odd or Even*. Or if she even needed to fit in.

"I'm in it too."

"*You?*" Artie stifled his guffaw, but I could tell he had it in him.

"I know it sounds stupid. But I think it'll work. We're probably not gonna say a whole lot." I thought better of that statement. "*I* don't know what we're gonna say. Or *not* say. And that's the whole point. I really don't want to talk about it so much."

"I get you. What's that Doris Day song? Que pasa, pasa."

"Sera, *sera*."

We convinced United Artists to let us shoot with a skeleton crew. We needed a sound man, a couple of grips and someone to help Artie with lighting and camera setup. I sold them on the idea that this was an intimate picture, a very delicate story, and that a big set full of technicians would be disruptive to our fragile young actors. I wanted to capture them at their most innocent and vulnerable, and you can't do that with carpenters and kibitzers around.

Jack Schiff, one of the producers at UA, fobbed his son off on our unit. "Kid needs to learn the value of work. He's lazy. Just show him what you want him to do and he'll do it." With those words, Owen Schiff entered our lives.

Maybe 20, blond, pudgy Owen seemed terrified of everyone and everything. He came onto the set when we had to gang-shoot all the scenes with Irene Ryan. She refused to go on location. She had health issues that made the wet, rustic climate of Oregon a no-no.

The first scenes of *Summer and Sandy* were shot on a soundstage in the Columbia ranch. I hate to admit this, because these were the first film scenes of my professional career, and they went 100% against my ethos. They looked like a TV show—you couldn't light those sets with any subtlety.

And I hated having to put the two actresses through this gang bang. We had one day to shoot six scenes. Two were long takes, with complicated camera moves, and crucial to the film. Irene Ryan was great. I'd never seen an actress get into character and stay there. It was like she pulled another personality over herself, like a suit of clothing. It was like her and unlike her. She was wasted on that damned TV series—everyone who loved her felt that way. But that rot hadn't yet set into her life. She *was* the aunt. Despite the railroad schedule, despite the sound-stage, despite Charlotte flubbing her lines and losing her focus.

After three bad takes of the same scene, Irene called me over. "Let me sit with Charlotte. I think she's self-conscious." She walked Charlotte over to a dressing room. I heard sobbing, screaming and laughter; outside the room, union technicians played cards and dawdled.

"Should I be *doing* something?" Owen had a bad habit of coming up on me, silent as the night, and scaring the crap out of me. His blue eyes watered like an old hound's.

I swallowed the urge to yell into Owen's face. "No. We're all on break right now. Until Miss Magill is feeling better."

"Is she *sick*? Should I go get a *doctor*?"

"She's okay. Really. Don't worry."

"Wull . . . Dad says I need to be *doin'* something. All the time."

"Your dad is full of crap. You're here to learn. And we learn by *observing*."

Owen was a husky blond version of Elisha Cook Jr. He had the same eyes and aggrieved, doubt-it'll-work-out expression.

The two women emerged from the cubicle. Charlotte seemed giddy and relaxed; Irene was relieved and ready to get going. They got through that first, relatively easy scene—character stuff, a non-essential exchange while doing the supper dishes that showed Lisa's dreamy attitude towards life and her aunt's skepticism. Yet she doesn't want to dash the girl's hopes. She's torn, and Irene got that subtle point across as she humored and gently corrected this headstrong innocent.

The big scene that day was the morning-after moment. Lisa comes home after Sandy deflowers her in a paint-smeared frenzy that destroys his portrait of her—the work he felt was his masterpiece.

The aunt knows exactly what's happened, and again tries her hardest not to fill her niece with guilt or shame—the two mistakes her mother had made with her. The aunt explains that she went through the same thing, when she was a girl.

Lisa has smears of paint on her body, and the aunt notices one of them. Irene did something beautiful with that moment. Watch the film and you'll see what I mean.

The last scene we shot that day was the first scene in the movie proper. Lisa arrives at her aunt's house to spend the summer. Her mother is in the hospital with some vague disease that's never defined. Lisa is used to the faster pace of the semi-large town she lives in, and worries that she won't fit in. She hits it off with the aunt right away. The older woman sees something of her lost youth in the impetuous, idealistic Lisa. And Lisa recognizes that she may have something to learn from this older woman, who's always been kind of a joke to the family because she never married. She was content to run a boarding house in this small town (which looked suspiciously like Mayberry or the hamlet of Petticoat Junction).

The scene called for one of the boarders to interact with the aunt—a good-natured alcoholic poet, he was behind on his room rent and tries to charm the aunt into giving him another break. I got Charles Lane, who was in everything, playing bit parts, and his brief scene seemed contrived on the set. I had him do the bit three times, and each take was identical. Not the slightest nuance. They looked fine on film.

I had some inserts of just Irene that needed to be shot outdoors, but we couldn't get to those that day. I asked her what her availability was like a couple of months down the road.

"I'll do it. I can always squeeze it in."

"Thanks. Great work today."

"Good script. That always makes a difference."

"Are we finished?" Owen took three months off my life. "Sorry to be asking questions again, but it looked to me like we were—"

"We're done for the day, Owen. Good work. Tell your father that I said you did great."

"But I didn't *do* anything . . ."

"You'll get the chance to do a *lot* when we're on location. Just get ready for that, 'cause that's gonna be some hard work. For *everyone*. And I'll really need you to be on your toes. *Okay?*"

He gave a sheepish smile. "Okay. Thanks, Mr. Jerome."

It was a big day for Artie, too. He had some help by a cinematographer who was hanging around the ranch, waiting on an okay for some future work. His name was Bob Hauser, and he did for Artie what Irene Ryan did for Charlotte . . . calmed him down, convinced him that he could shoot a professional picture.

He looked at Artie's storyboards for the morning-after scene and made a few suggestions that took about 60% of the grunt-work out of the shooting. I thanked him, and tried to slip him 50 bucks, but he declined. "Just killing time here. It was fun. I remember my first day on a real shoot."

I left the Columbia Ranch with elation. I'd crossed the border from gifted student film-maker to professional feature director. I had the thought that maybe shooting on sets, with scripts, wasn't an entirely bad idea. Movies needed more spontaneity and less gloss. There had to be some sweet spot of balance.

That day of shooting gave me focus about the ideas for *Never Odd or Even*. I realized that I needed this experience of coloring inside the lines before I could get all abstract and freeform.

Part of me still couldn't wait to turn a camera on and improvise a scene, with no idea where it would go, or what would be said. But a new part understood that complete chaos wasn't a guarantee of lasting art. The good stuff came somewhere in the middle. Freedom with a rudder. If that was possible.

TEN

The filming of *Summer and Sandy* taught me that the traditional way of movie making had its charms. Aside from bit parts played by locals, the story involved two characters—plus Aunt Myra, who never set foot in Oregon City but was cut into that footage to trick the viewer into equating those hard-lit studio backlot scenes with more natural on-location stuff.

My crew and I had a good picture on our hands. In Sam and Charlotte, we had two unspoiled young actors who worked well together in front of the cameras. Oregon City turned itself inside out to make our filming as smooth and comfortable as it could be. This didn't feel like my first feature. I was led to believe that a director's first feature was a pain in the ass—full of false starts, hardships and a learning curve steeper than a mountain.

Barrett Broadford deserves co-credit as director. He worked with the two leads, coached them on his words and how to deliver them, and then displayed the results to me before we shot a scene.

While he did that, Artie and I worked out the details for each scene's filming. We had solid storyboards, and having taken photos of the locations, we knew what we could expect from them visually.

Artie agreed with me that if we had strong natural light, we'd work with that—with soft key lights and a diffused spot to give the room a little extra illumination, so that it wouldn't look too shabby or dreary, which it was in person. In this compromise of my vision of film, I wanted as much reality as I could get—from the locations, if not from the script.

For all its flowery language and theatrical speechifying, the screenplay had a believable feel of adolescence. It got the way teenagers think they already know it all, yet are such larval things: so malleable, innocent and inexperienced.

The miracle of the picture was Sam. Whether Barrett had him hypnotized, or got him through rote memorization, Sam knew his lines and spoke them like he meant them. He embodied Barrett's idea of Sandy—the gifted artist able to express himself through paint and brush, but hard to reach on other planes.

I think Charlotte was in love with him. And though Sam was pre-occupied, the inevitable happened. They spent all their off-work time together. The sight of Sam's smile took some getting used to.

Another *amour perdu* made itself obvious: Barrett was smitten with Owen Schiff. He insisted that Owen be his "preparation assistant." Fine with me; it took the kid off my hands and gave him more to do than get coffee or clap the slate-board.

I had Owen assist the sound technician. He held the boom microphone when needed, did mike placement and sound testing. As filming went on, Owen developed a passion for sound engineering.

He did not develop a passion for Barrett Broadford. Our author grew sulkier with each day's shoot. He still coached Charlotte and Sam with warmth and devotion but was icy on the set. The chill was viral. Between takes, I took him aside and asked him what was wrong. Was he happy with how we were filming his screenplay? Yes, that was fine. Was he happy with the settings? Yes. The realism, the rural feeling was just right for his story. We were shooting in black and white. Was that right for the story? Perfect. Color would neutralize the human drama.

Well, then, what was wrong?

"I can't tell you. You wouldn't understand."

I understood. And I confess: I took advantage of Barrett's lovesick state. That kept him busy in the evenings, as Artie, Sam and I embarked on a cinematic experiment. We had two hours' worth of black and white film that was supposed to be ideal for low light and night shoots. Artie had a collection of fast lenses and aperture plates that he'd used on documentaries.

"It might look grainy," he warned me. Grainy, schmainy. Rough edges were what I wanted—or thought I wanted.

I had an idea for how to start *Never Odd or Even*. I'd discarded that original idea about staging a crime. It called for too much planning—too many people had to sign off on it and we'd lose our edge. We'd just wing it; see where the characters and situations took us.

It would start with the aftermath of a failed robbery. We couldn't stage the robbery without violating my thesis. I had Artie set up the camera and lights, and Owen ran the sound. To get into character, Sam and I ran the length of Main Street three times, back and forth.

Artie and Owen were to start filming and recording as we finished the run. I had a suitcase in one hand. Sam had a burlap bag. We were out of breath, sweaty and already tired from a day's shooting.

We stopped at a chalk mark drawn by Artie. Sam and I gasped. I looked behind me. Sam did the same. I coughed and lit a cigarette. Then I snapped my fingers. "The bag. The *bag*."

Sam gave me the burlap with a sheepish look on his face. I tossed my cigarette away and opened the bag. "Eleven *dollars*," I said, as I removed the money I'd dropped in the sack. "Eleven dollars and, and . . . sixty-eight *cents*."

"That'*sawl?*" Sam grabbed the bills away from me. He counted them. "*Twelve* dollars 'n' sixty-eight cents. Y' *missed* one."

"One extra dollar. Yeah, that's great. *Great*. That's what we almost got caught for."

"'Nough t' get some dinner. *That's* good. *Right?*"

"Great. We *eat*. But where do we sleep?"

Sam shrugged. "The car."

"The damn *car*. Curled up in that damned cold car. Crammed in there with you. You snore like a son-of-a-bitch."

"Well, you talk in y'r sleep. Up half the night from you whinin' like a baby. Like y'r havin a bad dream."

"Bad dream? It's a bad *life*. You said that store was easy pickings. 'Won't take nothing to crack.'"

"It *was*! But that was *last* night. I *tole* you that. Last night they might of had a thousand bucks in the till. I couldn't vouch for t'night."

Nature joined our improvisation. It began to rain. We moved, our pace speeding as the rain fell harder. I hoped Artie was getting all this. I guided Sam around a corner and shouted "Cut!"

We did another setup under the large awning of the post office. The rain drummed harder. Artie could only get us on one side without causing rain damage to the camera and lens. Owen huddled near us with the tape deck and mike.

Sam and I continued the scene. I was pissy; he was defensive. He argued that the idea was good, but that I didn't listen. And that was because I didn't take him seriously. I always had to be right.

I countered that I *had* been right—many times—and that I *did* listen to him. The conditions weren't right the previous night. Too many people. The police were close by. We'd have been caught.

"You're a damn *coward*," Sam said. He looked angry. "You're 'fraid of the cops. That's *poison*, man. You get scared, y'aint no good to *nobody*."

The argument built, and then real life gave us a gift. A drunk driver misjudged a turn and crashed into a mailbox in front of us. We didn't have to act: Sam and I were startled. Had the car been going faster, or at a different angle, I'd have been plowed down.

Sam crept around the driver's side of the car. He leaned in the window. "Hey, *mister*. Yew *awright*? Hey." He shook the man, who was dead drunk. "He's out. Well, *hell*."

Sam looked left and right. He reached into the guy's jacket pocket and extracted a wallet. He pulled out a stack of green. Then he tucked the wallet back.

"Sixty-three bucks." Sam beamed. "We ain't sleepin' in no car *t'nite*."

"Let's get out of here." I was shaken from the impact of the accident; I looked over my shoulder. A siren wailed in the near distance as it approached us. "Come on."

We ran into an alleyway—then right back to the equipment, which we all helped grab. We and our gear ducked back into the alley and watched the police and ambulance service arrive.

It was too dark to get reaction shots, or footage of the officers at the scene of the wreck. Too bad; those would have been great for the film. We stayed in the alley until the police left. By then the rain had simmered down.

It was almost midnight. We needed to sleep; we had a long day of shooting ahead. Artie and Owen saved the night's work in film cans and tape boxes, all labeled **NEVER SC. ONE**. Was it any good? I had no idea. But it was something shot.

It took a week for that film to get developed. While we waited, more of *Summer and Sandy* got in the can. Bad weather forced us to revamp one important outdoor scene—in which Sandy completes the portrait, and a few hours (in film time) before the traumatic seduction—to suit the lousy weather. Barrett's script had both characters marveling at how beautiful the day was.

"What will we *do*, Charlie?" Barrett erased replacement dialogue from his copy of the script.

"What if . . . we *keep* all that dialogue. But make it like a private joke between them. They *act* like it's a beautiful summer day, but it's . . ." I gestured to the downpour that drummed on the tin roof of our outdoor location. "We need a little comedy here. Because things are going to get so dark in the next couple of scenes . . ."

"Well . . ." Barrett bit the eraser off his pencil (by accident) and spat it out in disgust.

"Let Sam and Charlotte play with it a little bit. They know their characters. Let it be a . . . kind of an unspoken signal between them. That their friendship is about to cross over into another area."

"Huh." Barrett now bit the metal ferrule on his pencil. *"Huh."* He glanced over at our stars. "Let me have a minute?" I nodded. The three huddled. I heard laughter from Charlotte and Sam, who also let out an enthusiastic "Yeah! *Yeah!*"

I confabbed with the crew to get things set up. We'd do it as a single shot and film a couple of close-ups after the fact to punch up certain lines of dialogue. Owen sort-of helped Artie, then sort-of helped the sound technician. He tripped on a power cord and took a pratfall in the dry dirt. I helped him up. His nose was a little bloody.

The scene filmed itself. Charlotte and Sam stuck to Barrett's words, and worked in some ad-libs that brought just what I hoped to get for the scene. Sam cracked up in a way that I feared would be out of character, but once I saw the rushes, I left it in. That moment has become one of the indelible things about *Summer and Sandy*.

Charlotte, who had stuck religiously to the shooting script, had a gift for improvising. I felt Barrett wince each time she went off his words, but her interjections added to the richness of the moment. I wanted to channel this playfulness through the film. It felt more real and alive than any of Barrett's well-meant words.

And it occurred to me that Charlotte might have a place in *Never Odd or Even*—if she was willing.

Artie, Owen and I screened the rushes of that film's first footage in a downtown theater in Portland. It was the blunt, uncut footage, married to the unmixed, unbalanced soundtrack. "You don't talk about this to *anyone*. Okay?"

"Okay." Owen seemed shamed and grateful to be in on the viewing. I felt anxiety creep up my spine as we entered the empty theater. We found seats and I waved to the projectionist to run the film.

The lights dimmed. Countdown leader came into focus. There was no sound yet; just the muffled whirr of the projector upstairs. Then the leader ended. A crisp, in-focus night scene showed Sam and I, hands on thighs, breathless from our sprint. Owen's hands came into frame. His reluctant voice called the take and Sam and I got into character. I hit the mark; looked over my shoulder. Sam, two sprints behind me, did the same. I lit a cigarette. I looked tired and irritable.

"The bag. The bag." My voice sounded dumb. The sound levels were muddy. I hoped they could be balanced in the lab.

Sam got the Owen expression on his face. He gave me the bag. I threw my cigarette behind me. It bounced twice and rolled down a storm drain. *"Eleven dollars. Eleven dollars and, and . . . sixty-eight cents . . ."*

The footage lasted four minutes and thirty-five seconds. We ran it three times. It wasn't great, it wasn't terrible. The best part was the car accident. Artie picked up the stationary camera and did a bold hand-held move to reveal the smoking, hissing car. The shakiness reminded me of *Gun Crazy*.

The winning bit was Sam's pickpocket of the drunk guy. It was spontaneous, in character and true to who Sam was, on or off-screen. His look of delight, as he showed me the money, was perfect. That was real life, real feeling looking back at us from the movie screen. *That* was what I was after!

"This is gonna work, Artie. It's gonna work."

Artie looked like he wanted a cigarette, but he didn't smoke. He smiled. "I was so lucky to get that hand-held stuff okay. The picture looked good. *Didn't* it?"

"Was the sound okay, Mister Jerome? Did I get it *right?*"

I whammed Owen on the back. "Right on the money. *See?* You're *learning*! We can boost the sound quality when we put the film together."

Owen looked confident for the first time in our working relationship.

"Question." I spoke over my shoulder to Artie, who shared the back seat of my car with Owen.

"Huhm? What . . ."

"Do we let *Charlotte* in on this?"

"This what?" He yawned. It was way past his bedtime. "*Never Odd or Even*. You saw her today. She's good with ad-libbing."

"A crime picture needs a woman. It can't be all men. It'd be good for the movie. So . . . *yes*."

I stopped at a red light. "Do you think she'll *do* it?"

"Only one way to know."

I waited for the answer.

"Ask her. Now lemme *sleep*."

ELEVEN

We asked her the next day, after we'd stopped work on *Summer and Sandy*. I pitched it as an extension of the fun she and Sam had ad-libbing on top of Barrett's precious screenplay. Only it would be ad-libbing with the aim towards serious drama. We didn't use the words *film noir* then. "It's a hard-hitting crime drama. The first movie to show the daily lives of criminals. No Hollywood spin. Just the real thing."

Charlotte laughed. "But *I'm* not a criminal. *None* of us are."

I looked at Sam. His poker face didn't break. "You're not a teenager—no *offense*."

"None taken." She smiled at my *Dobie Gillis* reference.

"But you play one well."

"I was a teenager once. Not so long ago. It isn't a stretch."

I gestured in the air as I searched for words. "Right. Right. But you weren't—you *weren't* that character in *Dear Octopus*. That was totally theatrical. A complete fiction. No one like that character has *ever* existed in real life. How did you find a way to *that* character?"

"The *play*, silly. Dodie Smith. She created Fenny—and all the other characters. *She* knew who they were. And she got that across in her play. And, of course, the director helped me. Helped us *all* to find our characters . . ."

I took a nip of my cocktail. The subdued light of the lounge made me squint. It was some place called Howell's. "I think you could find your character. Only there won't be a script."

Charlotte looked concerned. "Why *not*?"

"I want you and Sam—and *me*—to ad-lib. You know, like Cassavetes. We have a situation and a location—that's it. We let whatever happens happen. If one idea doesn't work, we try another."

"Aren't you going to waste a lot of film this way?"

Artie cleared his throat. "Film is cheap. Talk is cheap. If we get a good picture out of it, who cares *how* it's made?"

Charlotte nodded. The idea began to sink in. She smiled as she weighed the pros and cons in her head.

We ordered sandwiches—Howell's was famous for them, according to their signage. A weary man took our order as if he'd soon face a firing squad.

"So . . . what's the idea? Is there a story?" Charlotte leaned forward.

"The story will find us. What we've got so far is: Sam and I are small-time crooks. Stick-up men. We're not very good at it, but it's all we know. We don't know the *why*. We just know that Sam and I are thieves. The life's got us in the dumps. But we don't know the way out. Not yet."

"So . . . what if my character showed them the way out?"

I nodded. "That's a possibility. There's no wrong answer to this question. But it needs to come out of our characters. What's the word? *Organically*."

"So, what's *your* character?"

These were the four most helpful words for the film. I hadn't thought at all about that. "Artie, take some notes." Artie had a pocket-sized notebook on him. He sighed and felt for his ballpoint pen.

"I'm . . . I'm Charlie . . . Charlie Howell. I was a big deal in my home town. Top guy in the senior class. I was a . . . I dunno . . . a baseball champ. I got a scholarship to college, but things didn't pan out. I . . . I started drinking and got a girl pregnant. So, they kicked me out of school . . . .

"I got drafted and had a hell of a time in the service. It broke me. All that ambition and joy I had before—it was all drummed out of me. I came back to society like a guy who'd been in prison. I couldn't find my place in the world. I couldn't hold a job. I tried hard to fit in, but I just . . . I *couldn't*. You getting this?"

"'*Just . . . couldn't*.'" Our sandwiches arrived. They were better than sandwiches you might make at home, but not by much. The toothpicks-with-olives were a nice touch, but a sandwich is always going to be two slices of bread with various crap in the middle. Mine was roast beef and Swiss with too much mayo. "Okay. So . . .

I'm the hometown hero, alone in a big city, and I can't make it. So, one night, I steal a car. Just to see if I can do it. And I drive 'til I run out of gas. I end up in another city. And I find a revolver in the glove compartment. It's loaded. I leave the car and start walking. All I have are the clothes on my back—and the gun. It hangs heavy in my coat pocket. And then I come across a liquor store. Guy's closing up, but I elbow my way in and stick him up. I get 400 dollars just for pointing a gun in an old guy's face."

"Keep going." Charlotte bit into her chicken salad on rye, which looked much better than my sandwich.

"So . . . I get a hotel room, and after a good night's sleep, I realize that a career has found me. I get cleaned up and I head out. I'm worried that the cops are looking for me. I have breakfast . . . get the local paper. There's a story about the robbery. But it's nothing. The cops have no lead, and it's called a petty theft in the paper.

"That night I hit a grocery store on the other side of town. The checker is so nervous I don't have to show my gun. I get another 100, 150 out of that. On the way back to my hotel room, I stick up a laundry service. There's another 80 bucks. No violence, no one's hurt. I've found my calling.

"I get some gas for the car and drive across the state line. And I keep doing this. Stop in a town, get a room, size up the local prospects, and for once in my adult life, my luck holds out. Maybe I have a near-miss with the local cops in one city. But I'm smarter than them. I'm on my toes. I have to be."

Charlotte enjoyed the movie she saw in her head. "Great! And how do you meet Sam?"

I shrugged. "Maybe . . . maybe we're both trying to stick up the same place. Say, a gas station. We throw one another off, and the attendant has time to call the cops. They show up and we just barely get away. We're both running for our lives. Sam sees a great hiding place and there's room enough for two. We're—I dunno—we're in a junkyard. Hiding under a rusted-out car. Flat on our bellies, trying not to breathe. The cops walk all around us with flashlights. They know we have to be in there somewhere.

"And I notice one of Sam's feet is sticking out where the cops can see it. So. I nudge him and whisper, *'left leg.'* He gets the message and tucks it in just in time.

"We lay there, smelling dirt and oil, until the cops give up. *'They couldn't be in here,'* one of them says. And they leave. And after a while, we realize we dodged a bullet, so to speak. And maybe Sam's grateful that I tipped him off about his foot. So . . . we just kind of stick together. We figure out some good two-man methods and make out pretty well for ourselves. But we have to keep moving. *That's* the secret. Don't put down roots. Down the highway to a new town.

"We're always on the road. And it gets to wear you down after a while. You just want to have a place of your own. Not to sit behind the wheel and drive through the night and start your routine all over in an unfamiliar city. It's like being a travelling salesman . . ."

"Or a musician." Charlotte had a twinkle in her eyes. Poor Artie took notes in silence. He bit his lower lip in his heightened state of concentration.

"So—there's a backstory. I just made all that up, by the way." Artie still transcribed. "I think you can stop now, Artie."

Artie returned to reality with a start. His pastrami on dark rye waited for him. He lit into it.

"That's how we'll work on this movie. Make it up as we go, based on what we know about the characters."

"Does this have a title?"

I told her the *Never Odd or Even* history. Some things puzzled her. "So . . . you're paying for a *title?*"

"*If* the movie gets finished. *If* it gets shown. And *if* it turns a profit."

Artie cleared his throat. "We don't want anything to go wrong with *Summer and Sandy*. That's the main thing. I'm, I'm sure Charlie will agree with me."

"Oh, no question about it. We've all signed contracts for *Sandy*. We're obliged to bring back a movie—a commercial picture that will make money. United Artists will sue us if we don't deliver. So that's a given. We complete *Sandy*."

Artie looked up at me with relief. I think I worried him. "I'm not sure this idea of mine will even work. The only way I'll know is to try it. If it doesn't pan out, then maybe I'm wrong. Maybe there's not enough room in the movies for realism—outside of documentaries." I shrugged and sipped at my gin and tonic. The ice had weakened it too much. It was bitter water.

Keeping Barrett in the dark about our experiment was hard as hell, but his infatuation with Owen helped. I checked in with Owen—sometimes hourly—about how he was holding up. "He's real *nice* and all." Owen couldn't look me in the eye. "A *real* nice guy. But he won't leave me *alone*."

"*How* won't he leave you alone?"

Owen blushed. "He just . . ." He gestured with his hands and forearms. "It's hard to *explain*. It's just . . . it's creepy. It's like . . . well, he keeps *tabs* on me."

I raised my eyebrows for more information. "Like, when we do the night filming, and I don't get in 'til real late, he hears me opening my room door. And I see his curtains part. He looks at me, then the curtains close and his lights go off. And then he's, like, all cold and snippety with me in the morning."

"I'll talk with Barrett. He'll listen to me. Just keep on doing what you're doing, Owen. You're learning about doing sound. You're doing good these days. I've told your dad." Truth be told, I hadn't. Nor did I persuade Barrett to ease up on the obsession. Because *Never Odd or Even* needed him to be distracted and unaware of its existence. It was a gut feeling; I could see him finding out about it and wanting to write a script for it. And, yes, getting snippety with me in the morning when I told him we didn't need a writer.

I didn't want anything to sabotage *Summer and Sandy*. It was a big break for me—for all of us—and if one little piece fell out of place, I'd be back to directing dog food commercials. Charlotte and Sam had a real chemistry. They made Barrett's stagy, self-important words seem warm and human. Their performances were a triumph over the naïve flaws of the screenplay. Without them, it would seem too obvious and *written*.

On the set, aside from his heated glances at Owen, Barrett was calm and collected. He might offer a different line reading, or gently correct the actors if they ad-libbed away too many of his precious syllables. I think he felt his work was in good hands.

We all went to Portland to watch 30 minutes' worth of unedited scenes of *Summer and Sandy*. Our shooting schedule—and Oregon City's lack of a screening room—kept us from seeing our work 'til then. Artie and I had put together the best takes of each scene we'd shot that had been processed. The footage lacked the gloss that it would get in the editing room.

It looked great. Artie had a clear idea of the movie's look and had gotten that across to our camera operator. The outdoor locations, with their raw autumn sunshine, driving rain and crisp nights, translated to the screen in a dense range of greys, blacks and whites.

But any film can look good. The *content* was what mattered. And though I winced at some of the screenplay's Tennessee Williamsesque turns of phrase—statements no living being *has* ever, or *will* ever, speak—Charlotte and Sam brought an intimacy to their conversations that made the worst twaddle sound convincing, and sold the best lines to the skies. These mismatched kids riveted my eyes to their actions, reactions and pauses. They owned the screen in that whirring, smoky projection room. If they could hold an audience in a real theater, we had a smash on our hands.

"I have an idea," Charlotte told me between takes of the scene that leads up to Sandy and Lisa consummating their relationship. We had a quick conference. She didn't want Sam to hear; she whispered her thought to me. I nodded in approval and admiration.

I had a surprise for our cast. Someone at UA had tapped Duane Eddy to compose a moody theme for the film, and his "Summer and Sandy" paired his twangy guitar with a string section and a tympani drum to create a yearning theme that really grew on me.

I got an acetate from the promo people and played it for the cast on a portable phonograph to set the mood. We heard it four times, to get it into our heads. "Think of this music, 'cause it's all over this part of the movie."

The moment came for Sam and Charlotte to take that first paint-smeared kiss. Both seemed shy. Sam's face turned red as he prepared. Charlotte's idea surprised him as the cameras rolled: she grabbed his paintbrush and daubed his cheeks with pigment. It gave him a grotesque appearance, and his response was to kiss Charlotte. Their lips met, and it felt real. Sam's paint got all over Charlotte's face. I wished I or Barrett had thought of it, but the scene was sexier and tenser for that little bit of business.

I hoped the scene would translate to the finished film with all that passion intact. Directing a love scene jarred me. I felt intrusive when I called "cut," or had to stop a scene so the actors could reposition themselves for the camera. We had three versions of Sandy's portrait of Lisa, all daubed with fresh, fragrant oil paint in case the tragic moment—when their passion destroys the painting—had some problem.

It went perfect in one take. There was no dialogue. The scene was lit in shadows, with a couple of key spots so the audience could see the painting, and the aftermath of the rolling and tumbling that maims the canvas.

On the set, the paintings looked freakish. The colors weren't natural—they were chosen based on what showed up in black and white with the best contrast. Lisa's face was a mass of hot pinks and greens. Her dress was an ugly orange, which looked rich and dark in the finished shot. Accents of hot blue and yellow, which would show up on the actors' clothes, made magnificent smears wherever they spread.

Notches cut in the canvas allowed them to rip in a controlled way. I'd instructed Sam on how to pull at the cut areas, and he got it just right in that moment where he straddles Lisa and her portrait, then claws at the painting to move it away and "tears" it right across Lisa's painted face. It made a ripping sound that shocked me and outclassed the work of any Foley artist. I had the sound editor bump up the volume on that rip. That shocked audiences in a scene that pushed at the boundaries of convention (and was chopped out of the prints in more conservative towns; I could write a book about that aspect of the film, but I won't).

We had another week of location shooting. And we hadn't yet tried another session on *Never Odd or Even*. Charlotte was raring to go and told me she and Sam had been working on their characters. "We have a surprise for you," she said. She wouldn't say more.

Fate dealt us a kind hand. Barrett was called back to LA to take care of his sick grandmother, to whom he was very close. With longing glances at Owen, our scenarist bid us a temporary adieu. We were free to film without fear for four nights.

"We're gonna take the savin's an' loan," Sam told me. He'd watched the local paper and learned of some big local fund-raising event that happened up in the hills of Oregon City. I never understood what it was, but all that mattered was the idea that the lowlands of town would be deserted—except for barflies who didn't give a damn about fund-raising.

We spent the morning and afternoon filming close-ups, reactions and a couple of re-shoots—none of it demanding work for anyone.

We called it a day, and after Artie and I huddled with the crew about tomorrow's shoot (more of the same, plus a couple of inserts we hadn't covered), we rested for a couple of hours, met for dinner and loaded the equipment into our two cars. It was a little after eight.

It was cold and damp. I could see my breath and Artie's glasses fogged over. We had our pick of a dozen good parking spots. Downtown Oregon City was deserted. We parked behind First City Savings & Loan, in the shadows, just in case a lazy patrol car made the rounds.

"It's too quiet." Sam looked up into the cloudy night sky. We heard a distant, muzzy high-school marching band—all thudding drums and blurting trombones—from somewhere on the hilltop. There, funds were being raised, drinks downed, hors d'oeuvres scarfed and small talk blathered.

"*Rolling*," Artie said. Owen carried the portable tape recorder and held the boom mike. We got a silhouetted shot of Sam, Charlotte and I creeping up the alley to the side door of the savings and loan. Charlotte laughed with surprise as Sam got the door open with the edge of a flathead screwdriver.

We entered and I shouted "Cut." The lights were still on inside. Nothing was put away. It looked like there'd been a fire drill, and everyone had forgotten to go back to work. A chaos of papers filled one desk; an electric adding machine, warm to the touch, buzzed as it awaited new input. Muzak played low and mediocre. A lukewarm cup of coffee sat to the left of the papers.

"Hello? Hey!"

No one answered Sam's shouts. The blinds were drawn, but all the lights were on. "There's enough light to film." Artie checked with a gadget from his pocket. "It'll look really high contrast in black and white. Very, uh, stark."

"That's what I want! All right, so let's get a setup here—maybe a little back towards the door, to get more of the room. The three of us, we're, uh, we just broke in and I'm . . . like, I'm not too happy that Charlotte's doing this job with us. I'm—"

"Jealous," Charlotte cut in. "Jealous 'cause you're kind of in love with me, and you think I'm too good for Sam."

"Yeah, and I, um, know that you got y'r eye on 'er. I'm startin t' rilly hate y'r guts cozza this."

"Great! That's all we need. So . . . let's all go about to this desk, and when Artie says 'rolling,' we start in towards the teller cages." I looked over my shoulder. This was exciting.

"Rolling," Artie said, and we ad-libbed our way through a comical scene based on the romantic triangle and what we had on hand. And what we had on hand was baffling. The teller cages were still full of cash and other artifacts of the workday. An egg-salad sandwich with the crusts cut off became part of the scene; we each took a bite from it. True to character, Sam doubled back to polish it off.

Charlotte seemed turned on by being with her two criminal men. Every comment she made had a Mae West kind of sexual aside to it, including a brief discourse on the phallic shape of rolled coins.

She found a paper in one cranny, unfolded it and laughed. She showed it to me. It had a crude cartoon, in red ballpoint, of a fat goose with a crabby face, horn-rim glasses and a trail of shit.

Underneath was the legend:

MISTER FINKEL
IS A GOOSE

I had no reason to doubt this. I did some business with Charlotte, and she kissed me on the lips. My surprise shows in the footage.

Sam and I siphoned cash and coins into cloth bank bags as Artie's camera shot us from behind the wooden bars of the rows of teller stations, arced around to where we were, and followed us into the savings and loan's vault.

The damned vault door was wide open. At that moment, I noticed the faint Muzak. It played a 101 Strings version of "Wonderland by Night." The vault was neat, and its rows of treasury-crisp bills looked like a Christmas present.

This was *too* good. I wanted to stop the scene, and the word "cut" was on my lips when Sam turned to me, alarm in his eyes. "This is a *trap*, man! This is *too* good! They're *onto* us! Les git the hell *outta* here!"

"But the *money's* here! Just like we planned. We can't leave it behind . . ."

Sam's look scared me. "We git the hell *out*. Right *now*. This is *bullshit*."

He pushed Charlotte into me. "*Really*, Sam. You trying to start something?"

"*No!*" Sam looked dead into the camera. "Move *out*! We gotta *go!*"

Artie and Owen doubled back—all of this was getting on film and tape—and Sam led us across the floor of the main room and out the side door.

The door slammed and an alarm went off. We were at the cars before Artie and Owen cleared the building. Outside, the alarm made a miserable, embarrassed tinkle. It couldn't compete with the muted marching band. No police sirens in the air; nothing but that bleached sound from a few miles away.

Artie and Owen placed the camera and sound equipment in the trunk. Once they scrambled into the car, I drove us out the back way and we took a ride over a bridge and onto a dark side road.

"So: Sam. What the *hell?*" I kept my eyes on the unpredictable road.

"I got a bad feelin'. Somethin' wadn't *right* there." He sniffled. This wet cold weather was getting to us all.

"*What* gave you a bad feeling?" Charlotte was half into her character. I could hear it in her voice.

"People jus' don't *leave* ev'rything out in the open like that. It gimme the *creeps.*"

"They probably went to that fund-raiser business. Got excited and everyone agreed to come back after and close up shop."

I heard coins jingle. "We got *us* a li'l fund-raiser too!" I felt the cloth sack at my feet crinkle as my heel touched it. "Holy shit!"

I pulled the car into a dark closed gas station. We counted the contents of the two bags. Ignoring the coins, we had about 500 bucks. "Shit."

"Guess that makes us real crim'nuls, huh," Sam said.

Charlotte laughed. "This is *wonderful*! Talk about *realism!*"

Artie sighed from the back seat.

"So, um, Ch-Charlie."

"*Yes*, Owen."

"So. Does this mean we're in *trouble?* 'Cos my father said that if I got in *trouble . . .*"

"Nobody has to know about this. Nobody saw us. This was a *fluke*. We can't go back and put it in the tills. How would we *explain* it?"

"Wull. We could, uh, put it in the night box."

"What?"

"You know. The deposit box outside the place."

I sighed. The kid had a point. We hadn't meant to take this money. Part of me felt that First City had this coming to them. They were careless and shoddy. This theft would be a lesson to them to be more cautious and professional. "What do *you* think? Sam?"

"*Hell*, no. We *earned* this. No way *I'm* givin' it back."

I felt something between a sigh and groan travel up my throat from the pit of my stomach. "Fine. I'll return *my* bag. Okay? *That* good with everyone? And then Sam's taking us all out for a real nice meal in Portland."

Voices murmured in general assent. I turned around in the parking lot and retraced our path to the basin of Oregon City.

I saw flashes of red before we crossed the bridge.

A cop in a red vest with matching octagonal sign redirected traffic from Main Street. The fund-raiser must have ended. Cars swarmed in the opposite direction. The police had sawhorses across Main Street. The block of the savings and loan was out of bounds.

While we waited for our turn, I saw a silent comedy in front of the building. An older, fat balding man with horn-rim glasses, all anger and pointing fingers was, no doubt, Mister Finkel. He upbraided a weak-chinned younger fellow, a plump 40-something woman and a shamefaced man his age or older. No audio was needed. The guilty three were in big trouble. The worst had happened. The good times were over.

"I guess Sam and *I* are buying dinner." I took the detour and we headed towards Portland.

We didn't have dinner in Portland. We settled for a Mexican place along Highway 99 East. As we ate tacos and enchiladas, I brought up the idea that we could use the bank robbery money to buy a lightweight Arriflex camera—the kind newsreels used—and continue *Never Odd or Even* on our own time.

I had access to low-cost film stock through my connections at UCLA. It wasn't ethical to use equipment and supplies that were earmarked for *Summer and Sandy*. We could get away with what we'd shot so far, but I didn't want United Artists to raise their collective eyebrows.

Artie lit up as I spoke. Charlotte and Owen were neutral. Sam seemed shocked, at first, but I could tell he was on my side before I stopped talking.

Portland had a couple of good shops that dealt in motion picture equipment. On our way back from the end of the shoot, we'd stop and buy one. A solid used model would spend our ill-gotten bankroll.

"We can film some more on the way back home. As the mood strikes us. Good?"

Everyone nodded and murmured assent. Sam belched. "It's this dang *beer*." Charlotte laughed and put her arms around Sam.

The next morning, we had great clouds and diffuse sun. We got a couple of long shots and casual scenes that could be cut into the movie as needed. We found a nice stretch of rural highway and Artie got some hand-held footage of Charlotte and Sam walking on the shoulder of the road, his arms burdened with a canvas and paints, her hands busy with a basket of wildflowers. A bridge over a rustic creek made another sweet setup. Up the road a bit, I spotted a general store. "Pull over."

"Artie, get some wild shots of the kids. Talking, laughing, chasing each other. Just get them to ad-lib. Owen, you're now my second unit director. You tell them what to do."

Owen got over his stunned feeling and took charge. They filmed outside and around the wooden storefront. I went inside and found a pay phone—the old-fashioned kind with the chessman-shaped earpiece. I dialed MAin 4-4464—a number I knew by heart.

"First City Savings and Loan. How may I direct your call?"

"Mister *Finkel*, please."

"May I tell him who's calling?"

"A. Crook."

"One *moment*, Mister Crook." I waited until a grouchy, wheezing voice answered. "This is *Finkel*."

"Mister Finkel? This is A. Crook. I robbed your establishment last night."

A dog-like sound—part whimper, part growl—buzzed in my ear. "I just wanted to call and tell you . . . Mister Finkel: you're a *goose!*"

I hung up and bought a round of Cokes for my cast and micro-crew.

We filmed into late afternoon, grabbed windswept closeups of Charlotte and Sam and re-filmed one scene that I felt we hadn't cracked the first time. We spotted a clearing shrouded by deep woods, and our cast nailed the scene in two takes. Charlotte and Sam worked together so well by this time that I wished I'd been able to reshoot about half the picture. But with a good editor, the movie would gel. The score, the mastering of sound and image in the labs and the marriage of the soundtrack to celluloid would make all this into a movie.

With the third take of the scene, *Summer and Sandy* wrapped.

Artie and I spent an hour poring over the master shot list, sure that we'd forgotten one important scene, but every shot had an X in the FILMED column and the RECORDED column. We logged the wild shots we'd gotten that day. Except for the scenes with Irene Ryan, which would be easy and fast, we closed the book on our production.

With Owen's help, I prepared all the exposed negatives for shipping back to LA, wired UA to let them know we were done, and organized the reels of magnetic tape that held our soundtrack.

On his own time, Owen had recorded a couple of reels of ambient sounds: birds, tree limbs rustling in the wind, night sounds of trains, coyotes and rainfall. These two tapes would create a distinctive part of the film's feeling.

"Owen, I have to lay it on the line. When I first met you, I thought you were an idiot."

"I *know*." He didn't (or couldn't) look up.

"You seemed like a stupid kid with no ambition and no calling."

"*Yes* sir."

I touched his chin and made him look at me. "*I* say that you're *not*. You're a really good sound man, and you handled the second unit like a pro today. I can't wait to see the shots you got."

"Aw, Artie really *did* it all."

"*Everyone* did it. Movies are a team effort. Everyone has a chance to put some part of themselves into a picture. It may be something that's their secret—that no one who sees the movie at their neighborhood theater would notice. But it's theirs. And there are parts of *Summer and Sandy* that are all yours. You did *good*!"

"Thank you, Charlie."

"I'm gonna use you on my next picture. And on *Never Odd or Even*—if you still want to be a part of that."

"Sh-sure."

The materials were insured and shipped to LA, and another wire to UA announced that the five of us would drive back to California. They could expect us back in two weeks.

TWELVE

On the way out of town, I bought that day's issue of the *Enterprise-Courier.* We were front page news—the story of the year. In the first screaming banner headline they'd used since V-J Day, the tale was told with drama:

MOCKING BANDIT ADMITS NIGHT-TIME HEIST OF LOCAL S&L
Shocking Telephone Confession to Thad Finkel, First City Savings & Loan Manager, of Monday PM Theft

The reporter took Finkel's word as gospel. They printed every sputtering, venomous word that came from his mouth. In a few paragraphs, the "mystery crooks" were referred to as *cads, monsters, scofflaws, hooligans* and my favorite: "defilers of our most sacred of institutions."

Local police had no hope of catching the "gang of thieves," but assured readers that First City S&L would undergo a total revamp of their security policy "to restore and ensure the faith of our valued customers and clients."

"Let's see how many newspapers we can *get* in." Charlotte's voice brimmed with glee. The story got a few dry chuckles from Sam. Artie and Owen had no visible reaction.

We bought a decent used Arriflex in Portland. Artie haggled with the shop's owner and saved us enough that we had money for a couple of lenses he really wanted. It was a good use for ill-gotten gains, and it gave me an idea. I couldn't bankroll the filming, but robberies would cover the costs if they were big enough.

I laughed aloud in the camera store. "I'll explain later."

I explained later, over lunch. "We didn't set out to commit a real crime, but we did. And thanks to that money, we have a camera, film stock and some new toys for Artie. We can continue to shoot *Never Odd or Even*."

"So now . . .?" Charlotte wasn't sure how to finish her question.

"So now we commit to being real criminals. To finish this picture, the robberies *have* to be real. And they *have* to be good enough to pay for film stock and whatever else the production needs. To finish this picture, we have to live the parts we'll play in front of the camera.

"If we get caught, that's it. Our careers are over. We serve time. If it's me, I do 10 years, get out, and if I'm lucky, it's back to shooting dog food commercials." I gestured to the young actors. "*You* get caught, you can kiss acting goodbye. Unless they have a theatre group in your prison."

Sam held his coffee cup to his face with two hands. "We won't *git* caught." He sipped.

"I appreciate your optimism. How do you know?"

Sam shrugged. "Nivver got caught yet. I'm *keerful*."

"But the most careful people *still* make mistakes. We're human."

Sam nodded *no*. "We know what we're doon. I size up the job forehand, make sure there ain't no trip wires. We don't do shit 'less I think it's good."

"So . . . *you* call the shots. In *my* film."

"Ain't *your* film no more, bud."

Owen spoke up. "Y-you *said*, Charlie; 'movies are a, a team *effort* . . .'"

Damn it, I *did* say that. I cleared my throat. "Okay. It's *our* film. But the original idea was mine. We're all working together to see *my* idea through." I tried to *ahem* again. I had a frog in my throat—a rising lump. "I trust you to know what will work. I don't want us to get caught. I just want everyone to keep this in mind. We don't want to get caught. It would be . . ." I swallowed and cleared the lump. "It would be bad for the film."

No one argued with that.

Albany, Oregon was the site of our second robbery. We shot some good footage as we cased the place. I paid tribute to *Gun Crazy* with a sequence of Sam and Charlotte driving, ad-libbing on their recent string of bad luck, and bitching about the downside of the criminal lifestyle. Artie shot it in the back seat; Owen and I leaned away from him so we wouldn't bump the camera.

Sam chose the bank we would rob. It had to have what he called "the three Ls"—location, loose security and lazy staff. He kept driving by the First Bank of Albany. Each time, he gave it a long, thorough look.

Sam (and I) went inside the bank and determined that it had a good exit from a second-floor fire escape. The bank occupied the ground floor of a distinguished 1907 building; various small businesses took up the three floors above. Artie and Owen followed us as we discussed our options for getting in and out of the place.

We went into the lobby, scanned the building directory and took the stairs up one flight. The hallways reverberated with our footsteps. Artie and Owen hung behind, which was best. You couldn't hear yourself think in these dense, shiny corridors.

I found the fire escape window at the end of one leg of the floorplan, next to an insurance company's lobby. The window was busted. The latch was missing parts and hung loose and useless. It opened but needed to be propped up. Without support, it sank like a shot. I just saved it from slamming shut with a huge racket.

Sam walked out onto the fire escape. It was old and rusty. It creaked a warning, but it held. Sam didn't linger. "She'll last long 'nuff for us to get down t' the ground. B'yon' that, I'da know."

I went into the bank to break a 50-dollar bill. The fixtures were old and frayed, but the room still had dignity. The vacant-faced, pudgy guard sat, lost in an issue of *True* magazine. "Ooh! A *big* one!" the teller said. He held the 50 up to the light. "Wonder if you'd find any of these in Grant's tomb?" I chuckled out of charity.

While I transacted with the teller, Sam scoped the room. I caught his movement out of the corner of my eye. I wondered if Artie was getting any of this on film.

The 50 was bisected into tens, fives, ones and a dollar in quarters. The teller got mixed up and almost gave me 51 dollars back. I pointed out his error. He laughed and took the bill back. Sam trailed me by 10 seconds. I looked around for Artie. I caught the glint of sunlight on the camera lens. He and Owen were restationed in the back seat of the car. Just like *Gun Crazy*!

I got behind the wheel. Sam followed in a moment. Charlotte beat him to the car and sat between us. He realized that we were on film.

"So. How's it look?"

Sam shrugged. "Old bank, old equipment. Saw a couple of big ullarms up on th' wawl. Just fer *show*, I bet. The guard's a *joke*. They pro'lly never got held up once. They wouldn't know whut t' do. S'long as nobody hits the ullarm. 'F I had more time, I'd git in there 'n' cut the wires."

"We got a way out. A good one."

"They never expect you t' go *up*. Long's we can git up them stairs fast, 'n' out that window, we're set. We need us a stick fer th' window. An t' finda hidin' place outside the bank. Some ky'na dodge t' throw em off."

"Some ky'na *dodge*," I repeated.

The dodge was the Clarion Theater. From the back of the bank building, which was a graveled parking lot, we'd go down an alley, through someone's yard, where trees and bushes would shelter us from view, and then out onto the street. The Clarion was half a block down the other side of the main drag.

The four of us went to the movies at the Clarion. They had *Six Black Horses*, an Audie Murphy Western, and two Chilly Willy cartoons. While the cartoons played, with their tooty music and exaggerated voices, Sam checked the exit door. He went out and the door slammed shut behind him. I waited a few seconds and got up. I walked to the exit door and propped it open. Sam slipped back in just before a fat usher made the rounds with his flashlight. Chilly Willy captured the usher's attention and gave us time to return to our seats.

"Perfect. We park the car in the alley here an we'll be gone 'fore the cops know their ass f'm their elbow."

"*Is* there a place to park?"

"*Shhh!*" A collegiate type shot us a mean look. He wanted to enjoy *Six Black Horses* in silence.

"I'll show ya. I seen this one already."

Owen and Artie, with their popcorn and licorice, were all set for motion picture entertainment. They didn't notice us leave.

The rear exit let out into a T-shaped alley. The short end of the T went out to the next street, where a group waited at a bus stop. The long branch of the T was open on both ends. It revealed the back of several neglected buildings, and an open paved lot where we'd stash the car. The cement pavement was cracked and gnarled with grass and weeds.

"If our cameraman can keep up with you, we're good." I worried about Artie. He was prone to sweating and panting from little exertion. Owen had youth and stupidity on his side; he'd do whatever I told him. Artie was one sprained ankle or leg cramp away from blowing the whole affair.

Artie and Owen wanted to see the whole movie. It took Sam to get them outside. He led them into the daylight; he had a solid grip on their jackets. "It was a good one," Owen said. He didn't put up a fight.

We stopped for Cokes on the way back; we guzzled the king-size bottles in the car. Owen let out the first belch; Artie followed. I had a party trick in such situations. As my belch reached its peak, I mouthed the opening words of Lincoln's Gettysburg Address. "Four scores and seven y . . ."

"Ya run outta *gas*," Sam sneered. The others laughed.

"That was pretty good, Mi—Charlie."

"Thanks. It's my fallback in case the movies don't pan out."

I parked in the Pay-Day Hotel's lot, which had last been swept during the Truman administration. Broken bits of metal and glass, alongside scraps of dirty, wet paper, littered the asphalt, which was cracked and pocked with potholes. The debris spread onto the cement breezeways.

Sam flung his empty bottle out the car window; it burst, and the shards clattered all around. "What the hell?" I cried.

"Oops." Sam smiled a fake grin.

"That's not funny. Someone could get hurt—"

"You want I should sweep it up?" Owen startled me for the thousandth time.

"No, no. It's not *your* mess." I sighed; Sam made a beeline for his room. Artie glanced down at the broken glass. He looked guilty. That was Artie's default expression.

"How's it look, hon?" Charlotte had slept in at the Pay-Day Motel, with its incongruous palm-tree-and-sleeping-Mexican neon sign. She watched a crappy black and white TV in-between naps.

"Perty good." Sam leaned across the bed to kiss her.

Sam swung the door to his room shut with a snap.

I had the adjacent room to myself; Artie and Owen shared a double further along the breezeway. We all needed some downtime. I walked to a Chinese place I'd spotted and had adequate lo mein. I picked up the local paper and some junk food at a mom-and-pop grocery across the road.

Back in my room, I looked at the TV listings. I noticed that *Cry of the Hunted*, a movie by Joseph H. Lewis, auteur of *Gun Crazy*, would be the 8:00 picture on one of the three channels my cruddy TV set picked up. I'd never seen it. It couldn't be another *Gun Crazy*, but I felt sure it would reward my effort to see it. I almost invited Owen and Artie to watch it with me, but this felt like a personal event. It was on TV; they were free to watch it in their own room.

Cry of the Hunted was far more eccentric than *Gun Crazy*. With a bigger budget, it couldn't escape the glossy touch of its studio, M-G-M. A dream sequence played like some of the artsy interludes in a Gene Kelly musical, and though some scenes were filmed on location, and made stellar use of the settings, others were obviously stage-bound and stylized as a silent German movie.

The performances were all "acting," especially Vittorio Gassman's. He brought aspects of the opera to his role as the charismatic criminal on the run.

What impressed me most was how filthy the characters became during the film. Every drop of sweat seemed to stain their clothes. They lived in a state of grime. That felt like the director's touch— his way to bring some down-to-earth humanity to a fever-dream.

Via the lousy broadcast signal, with lines, static and a rolling vertical—and the frequent commercial breaks—I didn't see the movie under ideal conditions. It was like reading a coverless, faded, mildewed paperback novel. You hoped the last page would still be there as you strained to read the grey, smudgy print.

It gave me one idea. You almost never see the main characters of a movie dirty or scruffy. A bank robber wouldn't have much opportunity to drop his shirts off at the dry cleaners. He'd probably keep wearing the same clothes until he got to a place where he could let his guard down, shave and take a shower.

Charlotte and Sam could do as they pleased, but I vowed not to bathe or change clothes until we got back to LA. Unless I had to, for unknown reasons, I wouldn't even change my socks 'til filming was done. This seemed central to my character. I thought about how it would be to not take the time to brush my teeth, wash my face or otherwise be socially acceptable and "pleasant." This would be a real stretch. I might occasionally delay bathing 'til mid-afternoon, but I was bred to keep myself clean. I'd have to fight against the urge; get used to my mouth tasting terrible, to my skin itching and flaking, to dandruff dotting my shoulders. If I got mud on my pants cuff, too bad. It'd have to stay.

A shot—or backfire—woke me in the middle of the night. Half-asleep, I walked barefoot out to the parking lot and stepped down hard on an upright shard of a broken Coke bottle. I recognized it as the one Sam tossed onto the cement sidewalk. *Well, there,* I thought; *that's my point.*

Then the pain woke me up; I lost my balance and stepped down again and the glass dug deeper into the center of my right heel. I fell to my side in a moment of shock after that pain.

I pulled the piece of bluish glass out of my heel. It was a jagged, deep cut. "God damn it, Sam," I said. But the moment of reflection was over. Blood seeped from the wound. I hobbled to my bathroom before the blood got bad. It soaked into the grouting of the tiles on the floor. All I had to work with was toilet paper. I kept light pressure on the wound until the blood clotted. I peeled off the blood-soaked porous paper. Some of it stuck to the wound. I wet a washcloth with warm water and dabbed at the wound until it was clean. The bathroom's behind-the-mirror cabinet had someone's forgotten box of tampons. I used three of those to ad-lib a bandage around the heel. I put a sock over the foot and hopscotched back to bed.

In the morning, the foot hurt like hell. It was mottled with red blotches and swollen, and the wound had bled through the sock-and-tampon dressing. I fell asleep on top of the covers, and my foot rested on the edge of the newspaper. Blood penetrated two layers of the newsprint. I was sweaty and jittery.

I fumbled for the phone on the nightstand and woke Artie and Owen. "I need you to come to my room. Like, now."

I heard them lumber up the breezeway. "I wonder if we're *fired*?" Owen asked Artie. Artie pounded on the door.

"It's open," I shouted.

"*Shut up*," my neighbor shouted back.

"What?" Artie's voice cracked.

"IT'S. OH. PEN."

"*SHUT. UP.*"

"Should I come in?"

"YES!"

"*NO!*" Something thumped against the wall on the other side of my bed. The impact caused a framed photograph of a bland landscape to crash down behind the bed. The glass broke.

"Oh my *God!*" Artie turned pale.

"Mister . . . *Charlie!* What's *wrong*?"

I told them. "I think we better go to an emergency room. But in another town."

"But why . . ." Then Artie got it. We didn't need to leave behind any evidence of our time in Albany. It would be bad for the movie.

I called information and pretended to be a ways outside of Albany, more on the Washington side than California. "You're near Corvallis," said the operator. "I can give you some addresses that are close by. Do you need an ambulance?"

No, I didn't. With Owen as my sentient crutch, I got into the back seat of the car. Artie drove the 17 miles like an old man. "You okay back there?"

"Yes."

"Too bumpy?"

"It's *fine*."

"Should I—"

"It's *fine!!!*"

The hospital looked like a post office—a blocky white building with a small sign you had to get up close to read. Maybe they didn't want a lot of business. We drove past it four times before Owen spotted the address.

Owen helped me to a wheelchair at the entrance and I squeaked myself to the front desk. "We'll wait in the car, okay?" He left without an answer.

After I explained my reason for being there, I had to fill out a pile of papers, despite my protestations that I was just passing through, was paying cash and would never be here again for any reason.

Three hours of waiting later, my aching, swollen heel was inspected by a balding doctor. "Mm." He probed the wound with a cotton swab. It hurt. "*Mm*." He soaked a wad of cotton with alcohol and daubed at the wound. *That* hurt. "Mm."

"*Mm?*"

"Yeah. We got a deep cut here. Could get infected. Very easy for this type of wound. We'll get you bandaged up, but then you gotta stay off this foot. Only walk when you *have* to. Like to go to the can."

"Can?"

"Latrine. Bathroom."

"Right."

"You need to stay off this heel for at least two weeks. I'm gonna write you a prescription for an ointment. And you need you some gauze bandage and tape. But first . . ."

He dressed the wound. It hurt like hell, but it had to be done. I couldn't put my shoe on over the dressing. Then he wrote the prescription. All this cost me 48 dollars and the better part of a day of my life.

"Do you need help getting to the pharmacy?" I nodded yes. A miserable-looking woman, bony like a bird, appeared with another wheelchair and gave me a life-threatening ride to the lobby Rx. The ointment cost four dollars.

Artie and Owen sat in the car, their backs to me. I saw their silhouettes: hands moving to and from their faces. They were eating.

I wheeled out the automatic door and buzzed down the inclined walkway. Thank goodness no cars were coming. I bumped into the back of our car. The impact made Artie cry "What?" and caused my foot to hurt like a son of a bitch. "*Ow!*"

Owen turned around and looked shocked. He bumbled out of the car. "Mis . . . Charlie! Did you *hurt* yourself? You all right?"

"Just get me in the car."

"I can call a doctor . . ."

"Get me. In. The. *Car.*"

Owen supported my weight and I flopped onto the vinyl seat. An embarrassed Artie polished off a barbecue sandwich. He licked his saucy fingers, his cheeks like a chipmunk's. The residual smell of the sandwich reminded me: I was starving. "I'm starving. Take me to some food."

"Mm." Artie struggled to chew and swallow his mouthful of meat and bread.

French fries and hamburgers, coleslaw and a dill pickle, topped with a chocolate shake, helped me become a human being again. "Well," I half-belched.

"Yeah." Artie stole fries off my platter.

"You can have 'em all. I'm done."

"They taste better when I *steal* 'em."

"You're getting the criminal bug."

"Yeah." Artie cleared his throat. "So . . . your *foot.*"

"What did the doctor say?" Owen looked so sincere it hurt.

"I can't bear weight on the heel for at least two weeks. I run the risk of infection. I could lose my foot if I'm not careful." (I made up the last part for shock value.)

"Jeez." Artie snuck a fry that was legally his off my plate.

"So . . . what does this do to the film?"

"Yeah," Owen echoed.

The film! Nothing like pain and drama to take your mind off work. "Well, it means I can't be *in* the film. But Charlotte and Sam still can. They're much better actors, anyway. *I'm* not a movie star."

"So . . . what about the stuff we've already shot?"

"We'll figure it out in editing. That's where we'll find the story."

"I think we should all sit down and talk this through." Artie reached for a French fry. He'd eaten them all. He got an index finger full of ketchup, which he wiped on the tablecloth.

"We c'n do it." Sam sat on a small couch, his arm around Charlotte. She smoked, which shocked me. Maybe it was part of the pact she took to be involved with Sam.

"This gives me the chance to really *direct* the film." I waved away Charlotte's smoke. I was trying to quit. I chewed a giant wad of Wrigley's spearmint. "I won't have to worry about whether we're getting coverage." I glanced at Artie. "I mean, I *know* we're getting good coverage—" I patted Artie's shoulder for friendly emphasis— "but I'm no actor. I don't belong on the screen. *You* two . . . you've got it. You can make this movie work."

"So, this makes me a *criminal.*" Charlotte pondered that idea as she smoked. "Well, a good actress never turns down any role, as long as it challenges her."

"Mist . . . um. *Charlie.*"

"*Owen.*"

"Um, when this movie is all filmed and edited, and, um, gets shown . . . won't these guys be, like, wanted for a buncha *robberies?*"

"They might."

"I mean. When the other picture comes out, if it's a big success, everyone will reccanize them, right?"

I sighed. "Maybe. *Look.* We'll cross that bridge when we get there. It'll take me a year—maybe two—to cut the movie. I'll have to do it in my spare time. I'm sure *Summer and Sandy* will do well, and United Artists will want us all to work on a new picture."

"This could be wunna them ort house jobs." Sam stubbed out Charlotte's cigarette for her. "It ain't gonna be no A pitcher. Not 'less it turns out real good."

I nodded. "Crown International is interested in it. But only if they like it. Maybe it'll never get released. But it's a movie I've got to do. Just to prove that I can make a movie without a damned script . . . without a studio . . . without all the crap that comes with the system.

"Maybe it won't work. Maybe we've been wasting our time. But I want to do it. *Humor* me. You're all taking part in a great experiment. We won't find a cure for cancer, but we might stumble onto a way to make movies better. It could be good for the future of our business."

Murmurs of assent surrounded me. I had won them back.

Sam, Charlotte and I spent the next morning and afternoon plotting the robbery. Artie and Owen filmed us. This was an essential part of the job, and a staple of heist movies. Here it was, happening as we spoke.

We sat around a table in the motel's meeting room. The Kiwanis Club did their monthly get-together there and the room was decorated to suit their needs. Sam brought butcher paper and a china marker. He sketched out a rough floor plan of the bank. "Teller cages are *here* . . . that fat-ass guard sits *here* . . . there's wunna them *rope* things . . . people line up in that an' wait their turn . . ."

"How will we take care of the *guard?*" Charlotte looked intrigued.

"You c'n go over n sweet-tawk 'im . . . keep 'im d'stracted. Ast him about his work. Get him tawkin'."

"You got a piece?" I asked.

Sam looked at me funny. I made a finger-gun with my hand. "Bang bang."

"We doan *need* that trubble."

"But every robbery I've—*we've* done, we've had a gun . . ."

"Not no *more*. They're bad fer bidness. You c'n go a long way with tawk, long's you say the right words."

"When did *you* come up with this idea?"

"It's wunna the rules. Y' doan use guns. They catch you with a gun, you get the book th'own at you. *Hord.* I seen it happen."

"I just . . . I don't want you to get caught."

"Ain't gunna *happen*." Sam returned to his sketching.

"You forgot the check stand thing." Sam shot me that look again. "The . . . that big *block*. It has deposit slips. Pens on a chain . . ." I couldn't remember if that area had a name.

"Oh. Yeah." Sam drew a crude rectangle under the stanchion

rope's Z shape. Then he drew dotted lines to indicate the entrance and exit. He ran down his idea of going upstairs, and out the broken window, with Charlotte.

"Very *smart*." She kissed Sam on the cheek.

He continued with the idea of going down the rusty fire escape and through the alley to the movie theater. He would toss the money into the vacant lot where our getaway car was parked. "We gotta pra'tice this port forehand. Whut time'zit?"

"We're out of film." Artie set the camera down.

"Lunch!"

After lunch, we went to the bank. I almost stayed in the car, because of my damned foot. But I couldn't resist being there. Owen helped me; we got in without much notice.

Sam wanted to time the escape, and to see if it would work best with or without Charlotte. Sam got in the long post-lunch line and, after three- or four-years' wait, bought a money order. The slow line gave him time to scrutinize the teller cages, the layout of the bank lobby and the ability of the armed guard to respond to a crisis.

The crisis was an inflated paper bag, which Owen popped, on cue, in the foyer that led to the stairs and the bank lobby. The guard didn't notice the loud, echoey bang. He was too taken with Charlotte. She put on an exaggerated Deep South accent—almost a female Huckleberry Hound—and distracted the guard (whose name was Clarence) with chit-chat about *this wondaful tay-own* and its *de-laht-ful pee-pul.* He was an easy mark for her vaudeville belle of the ball routine.

"If we could just bring the camera in here."

"Huh?" I looked at Artie.

"I read about newsreel guys during the war who got footage they weren't supposed to get. This trick they did."

"Yeah?"

It was designed for desperate shots—moments that were news, but beyond the boundaries of politeness or consideration. They hid the camera in a suitcase or trunk, with holes bored for the lens. They had a sliding cover piece so the lens could be concealed before whomever got wise.

"Huh." Robbing a bank in the name of cinema art took plenty of nerve. Having a camera inside the building—not waiting in the getaway car—would be really gutsy. "I wonder how the picture would look?"

"Shaky." Artie nodded in regret. "But real. That's what you want. *Right?*"

"And the sound?"

"Owen could have the recorder in a satchel or attaché case. We can pin the mike under his lapel or something. With all the echo in here, sound won't be worth crap anyway."

I patted Artie on the shoulder. "Let's get a suitcase."

Sam got his money order and left. Charlotte had Clarence the guard on cloud nine; we left her there to flirt. Owen waited in the lobby and shot me a *what do I do now* look. I couldn't go up the stairs. By the time Artie climbed them, Sam was out the window and on the ground to the alleyway. Artie came down, huffing: "If we could get the camera up the stairs after him . . ."

"We have to play it by ear. I can't believe we're doing this."

Charlotte may have been the first female to pay positive attention to Clarence in his life. He was ready to make small talk with her 'til the end of the banking day.

Owen helped me into the car, and we drove around the corner. As we approached the theater, Sam waved from the alley to the left of the box office. I leaned out the window from the back. "How'd it go?"

"Four minutes. Mebbe three, an' I'll be in my seat, watchin' the show. Mebbe watch 'er twice. I'll cawl th' motel when it gits dork."

"We need to figure out what to do with Charlotte and Owen."

"He kin come with you boys. Shorelet, she kin mebbe keep tawkin' t' the guard. She c'd be a witness t' the whole thing. Give'm wrong in'famation 'bout the robber." Sam smiled at the thought.

We went back and gathered Charlotte, who seemed sad to stop her conversation with Clarence. "He's really a charming fellow. He writes *poetry*."

"How about *that*." Artie drove, with Sam and Charlotte scrunched beside him in the front seat. Owen shared the back with me. It made my ride less comfy—I couldn't stretch out my leg—but I wasn't in serious pain.

The last piece fell in place on the way back to the Pay-Day Motel. Owen noticed it. "There's a bus line from town." He spotted the signs for the local Route 17 along the highway.

I leaned out the car window. Three people waited at the stop. "Does this bus come from town?"

"'Bout every half hour," a wrinkled duffer said. "It runs slow sometimes."

"How late does it run?" He started to shrug, and the hiss of air brakes startled us both. Route 17 had arrived. The passengers boarded. "Get a schedule," I commanded Owen.

He just stopped the louver-style doors as they closed. "'Scuse me. '*Scuse* me. D'you have a *schedule*?"

"Every half hour." The driver seemed annoyed.

"When's the last bus from town?"

The driver cleared his throat of major mucus and spat at the highway. "10:15 weeknights, 9:10 Saturdays. No bus service on Sunday." With that, he hissed the door shut, adjusted his clip-on bow tie and hit the road.

Great: Charlotte and Sam would be able to get back to the hotel, together or separate, on their own.

With that final bit of info, we were set. I recited the duties in the car: Sam would commit the robbery while Charlotte kept the guard hot and bothered. I would, if possible, be at the check stand in the lobby with a deposit slip. Artie's suitcase-cam would capture the theft on film, as would Owen's portable sound system.

We drove again to Corvallis and found Stanley's Luggage Center. We dropped 75 bucks on a Samsonite suitcase, a large brown leather satchel and a wooden handled umbrella. "Cane," Artie whispered. It took me a minute to get what he meant. I tried the umbrella. It supported my weight fine, and its tip was covered with rubber, perhaps to prevent Three Stooges-style eye pokes in crowded elevators and subways.

I assumed Artie knew the sizes of the camera and tape deck. He chose both bags with confidence. "Going to New York City," Artie said to the dull-faced clerk. "I think I've landed a big job!"

The clerk nodded without interest and took our money. Artie handed me the satchel and umbrella. It took me several steps to get used to the walking stick, but it allowed me to move forward without killing my heel. My foot throbbed like a heartbeat. It didn't hurt, but the threat of pain kept me uneasy.

We walked around the corner to where the car was parked. Owen, Charlotte and Sam sat in the shadows. They put the luggage in the trunk. Without another word, we doubled back to the Pay-Day.

Sam and Charlotte beat feet for their room. I used my umbrella-cane like an old pro. An image of Lionel Barrymore came into my head. I almost imitated his voice, but this was no time for jokes.

Samsonite is a bitch to cut through without real tools. I had hammer, sandpaper and some Philips-head screwdrivers in the car. Owen offered a Swiss Army knife that was sharp, but not quite up to the task of this tough, rubbery fiber board. After much gouging, pounding, breaking of screwdrivers and improper language, we got a hole big enough to seat the lens. We bunched motel towels in the bottom of the suitcase. The camera could rest without too much jiggling or jostling.

I couldn't help the safety of my foot; as we worked to make the hole, I whacked my heel on the floor, which hurt like holy hell, and put pressure on it. You get into the groove of an activity and forget you have problems.

As I tried to even out the peephole, Owen's knife blade snapped off. He reacted like Claude Jarman at the end of *Ol' Yeller*. "My *dad* gave it to me." From the sad way he said it, it felt like this was the only gift he'd ever gotten from his hard-to-please Pops. I assured him I'd buy a new one—top of the line—once we were done with the film shoot.

The tape deck fit into the satchel. It had a long strap. I slipped it over Owen's neck and the strap rested on his right shoulder. "Not too heavy?"

"It's fine M . . . Charlie." Owen gave his approximation of a smile. I ran the mike cord up Owen's sleeve and stuck the microphone head into his shirt pocket upside down. He turned it on and closed the satchel flap. "Sound rolling."

I hobbled into the bathroom. Artie followed me and we ad-libbed a conversation in normal and loud voice tones. The loud version made the neighbors shout "SHUT UP!"

We played back the tape. It wasn't crystal clear, but it worked. You could hear what we said. The *SHUT UP!* picked up fine, which made us all laugh.

With that, we called it a day. After Owen fetched some adequate Chinese take-out from the joint down the road, which we enjoyed on my bed while Sgt. Bilko swindled a new mark, we said g'night and settled in for a good night's sleep.

Tomorrow, we'd try this thing out. We'd have a great scene, or we'd all end up in jail. Or both.

THIRTEEN

We left the motel at ten, drove our caravan to a pancake house, and fueled up for the day's adventure.

"Should I be . . ." Artie looked back at the trunk of the car, with the camera and sound equipment.

I got his drift. "No, no. You need to eat. Save that for when it counts."

Sam and Charlotte had a table waiting when we came in. "So. Pancakes all around?" I waited for an answer.

"*You* c'n have all y want." Sam cleared his throat. "Plate fulla them thing's'll put ya t' sleep in an hour. Not good f'r our line'a work."

Sam had eggs and bacon, plus all the coffee and water he could wash down. The rest of us followed suit. Owen looked disappointed, but he didn't say anything.

"We can have all the pancakes you want after."

"If there *is* an after."

"And why *wouldn't* there be?"

"Well . . ." Owen was ready to rattle off a long, itemized list of reasons why today's adventure would and could go wrong. I didn't want any morale loss at our table.

"You've got to take a more *positive* look at life, kiddo. Hope for the best and don't get *depressed.*"

Owen looked appalled at me.

"Don't make me sing about the rubber tree plant. Because I will."

And I sang: *Next time you're found with your chin on the ground, there's a lot to be learned, so . . .*

"Okay *okay*! I *hate* that song!"

Charlotte complemented me on my singing voice. Artie looked like a car had hit him; Sam was without words or obvious reaction.

We ate in silence, aside from grunts of "pass the salt" or "more coffee." Everyone was afraid I might burst into song again.

We drove toward the bank. Sam and Charlotte took the front seat. Artie, Owen and I wedged in the back. Artie had the camera out of the suitcase, and he filmed a further homage to *Gun Crazy*. In character, Sam and Charlotte ran back over their strategy: she'd keep the guard distracted while he did his business.

"You stay put with fatso in there. Don't worry 'bout me. I'll git outta there an' go into hidin'. Got it timed. Even if they find me in the theeter, ain't gonna be more'n five bucks on me."

"I can't wait to read more of Clarence's poetry. You wouldn't understand it. But it's good. He's wasted in that job."

"Yew ain't gittin sweet on that lard-ass—"

"He's an *artist*. And he has a *glandular* condition. He said it happened . . ."

"We're here." Artie moved the camera around and bonked me in the head. Sam parked the car.

"And *cut*. Let's set up for the suitcase shots." Sam and Charlotte stayed put. Artie and Owen opened the trunk and did their thing. I heard shifting, thumping, squeaking and the final click of the suitcase latches.

Artie knocked twice on the glass of the rear door. I slid out of the car and struggled to my feet. My foot throbbed—a beat that also pounded in my neck. My umbrella cane was a huge help. "So how you wanna handle this?" Artie had the suitcase on his shoulder. I could tell it was heavy.

"We follow them in . . . actually, let me go in first and get a sense of how busy the place is. How much film you got in there?"

"Ten minutes, tops."

"We don't want to run out of film before the, uh, event is over. So. I'll signal you when it looks good. See me wave, then everyone gets in there. You-all ready for this?"

Nods, grunts of assent and a "yes, sir" from Owen.

"Park the car, Charlotte." She nodded and saluted. As she slid into the driver's seat, Sam got into character. He backed into the shadows of the bank building and combed his hair in a different part. He spritzed it with a travel-size can of hairspray so the new part would hold. Then he put on a pair of horn-rimmed glasses. He stepped into the harsh sunlight and he looked different. The changes were simple, but they'd make it harder to ID him if worse came to worse.

Charlotte rounded the building on foot. *"Fait accompli."*

"Okay. Everyone ready? Here goes nothing." I hobbled up the stairs, through the open doors and into the bank lobby. I felt anxious.

Clarence the guard, perched on his stool, scanned the local paper. A gaggle of elderly church ladies gossiped in a sunbeam. I wanted to throw them some chicken feed.

The line was short. One person stood at each teller cage in mid-transaction. A couple of people worked on their deposits at the desk area. This was it.

I tapped on the plate glass window and waved. Artie spotted me. He said something to Sam and Charlotte, turned the camera on, and trailed them as they jogged up the stairs. Owen fumbled with his satchel. I hoped he'd turned on the recorder. Charlotte made a bee-line to Clarence as Sam butted ahead of some local yokel who was about to step up and do business.

"Clay-rance! Ha-yow *good* to *see* you a*gain."* Charlotte's loud voice drew all attention her way. Clarence blushed and folded his paper.

The group of biddies laughed. This gave them a new world of material! Artie had the camera at stomach level now and panned across the room. I was out of camera range; I could point him to what I wanted to get on film.

One of the teller's windows opened and Sam stepped up. I got Artie's attention. He walked towards the edge of the desk. At that moment, Charlotte burst into theatrical laughter. She patted Clarence on the shoulder.

It gave Sam a perfect cover for the stick-up. He didn't need a gun. I wish I could have seen him work close-up. I wish the film could've gotten it big as life. Whatever he did gulled the teller. Sam moved his left arm once. The teller walked off-camera stage left. He came back with a fabric sack. Sam backed off and went for the stairs.

Artie panned and followed Sam up the stairs. "Cut. Get outside before there's a panic. Get me footage of Sam getting rid of the money and going to the theater. Go!"

Artie and Owen just got out the door before the alarm went off. The group of biddies gasped as one. "Ladies and gentlemen, we've just been robbed," a man, who I guessed to be the manager, shouted.

This news surprised Clarence, who reached for a gun he'd probably never used. His hand stopped; the act was futile. Charlotte gasped in shock. The camera was gone but her performance went on.

"Please stay where you are. Miss Ronson, close the lobby doors." One of the tellers waddled out and kicked the rubber stoppers away from the doors. They slammed shut. Sirens approached the bank building. In concert with the stale clang of the alarm, it was cacophony.

A minute had passed since Sam got out. Maybe by now he'd stashed the money. I imagined his slow walk down the alley to the theater. I pictured Artie tripping on loose gravel—falling face-down on the ground. Or Owen getting the microphone cord caught on a tree branch. I always figure if you picture the worst, when something good happens you're twice as happy.

Police sauntered in, their gait casual and unconcerned. "Jensen! What *gives*?" the main cop said to the manager. I couldn't hear them above the murmur of the dozen people in the lobby. The old gossips vibrated with tension. They had the scoop of the year and they couldn't get to their phones fast enough. I again thought of throwing them some corn and laughed out loud.

I didn't get out of the bank for an hour. The police lined us up and asked what our business was there. They shooed the gossip clique out; their reputation preceded them.

I had a good story—that I'd injured my heel and was detained in town to avoid infection. They called the hospital and verified that I'd been treated for the injury described.

I thought against telling them my real story. Once they saw the California driver's license, I spilled the beans. I was a film director who had just completed principal photography on my first feature, which would soon be released by United Artists.

I began to bore them with the details. I recited what lenses we used on certain scenes, and how to backlight actors; I made it clear I could continue for hours. "Hope your foot heals up real good," one cop said and they let me go.

I looked over my shoulder. Charlotte had an audience of two cops as she told a dramatic story. Her hands danced in the air as she described the robbery. I heard her mention the robber's harelip. I smiled as I walked past the cop in charge of letting people out.

I hobbled down the stairs and caned my way down the side street until the dirt road that led to the alley.

I expected the area to be crawling with police. It wasn't. I made my turtle pace up the alley, then turned right at the T. I got to the car. It was there. The engine was still warm.

The burlap sack was under the floor mat by the brake and gas pedals. I opened it and saw a thick stack of green—new bills, which bothered me, but it was a nice bundle.

I was in no condition to drive a car, but I had to get the thing out of the area. I couldn't avoid the pain of pressing down on the pedals. Back then, they didn't have a pain meter. No little row of cartoon faces. Mine would be the crying, miserable one at the end of the line. I took deep, rapid breaths. I scrunched my eyes closed and felt sweat trickle down my neck and back. I couldn't black out. It tempted me; I was exhausted, and the pain seared through me. If I could get the car a few blocks away, maybe in a pay lot, it'd be safe there overnight.

I started the car and turned left down the alley. "*Hey!*" I jolted with fear. I looked out the window. A delivery van backed towards me. It screeched as its brakes ground to a halt.

"Gotta go the *other way*," the van driver shouted.

"Gotcha. Okay." I put my car in reverse and backed up to the T of the alley. I felt nauseous from the pain. Throwing up wasn't good. I could do that at the motel. I rallied myself for the hardest work I'd ever done.

I got the car down the alley to the street. I looked left and saw the bus stop. The movie theater was across the street. Sam was in there. He had to be.

No police. I looked both ways and drove forward. Some kids darted in front of me. One bounced a basketball. I hit the brake. I thought I'd black out again but I took in big drafts of air, in and out, in gasps, and I recovered.

Three blocks down, I found a pay parking lot. I gave the attendant four dollars and the car was legally and safely parked until 1 PM the next day.

"You okay, buddy? You look kinda pale."

"Oh . . . I have a migraine. Just hit me. I'll be okay."

"There's a Rexall's on 8th and May." He pointed and I made out the cursive logo on the sign.

"Thanks. I can get something there."

With great effort, I got out of the car. I locked all the doors. The fabric sack of money tucked inside the armpit of my jacket. It looked like I had a tumor, I'm sure.

I was afraid I'd drop it in front of the attendant. He stood close by, unsure what to do. I got my umbrella-cane and was able to walk. I smiled and nodded. "I'm going to be all right."

"Hope you feel better, mister." I thanked him and walked off. "Mister! *Mister!*"

I turned and saw him run towards me. I fought the urge to run; I couldn't. He gave me a pink cardboard ticket. "Your *receipt*. Can't leave the lot without it."

"Oh, gosh. *Thanks.*" I put the ticket in my shirt pocket. "Well, here *goes* . . ."

The attendant said something I couldn't hear. I waved and hobbled away.

I made it to the Rexall and sat in their small lunch counter. I ordered a roast beef sandwich and a malt. "What a *day*, huh?" I said to the counterman. He looked back with a dull *no comprende* expression. "The bank robbery!"

"*What,* now?"

I told him the story, based on my first-person experience. I described the robber as tall, blond and stout. He had a Thompson sub-machine gun and spoke with a German accent.

"How much did he get?"

"I think a quarter million. I could be wrong."

My sandwich and malt showed up fast and he got on the horn to tell everyone he knew what he'd just heard.

I ate, had a coffee and settled up. I asked for a big glass of water and a tin of aspirin. I took five of those, downed the glass, and walked back to the restroom.

I went into the stall and latched the door. I sat on the lid of the commode and opened the burlap bag. The money slid out and I counted it: $6780.00 in tens, 20s and 50s. Most of the bills were new, but over $1000 were in old, mismatched currency. We could circulate those bills without worry. The new bills were sequential and could probably be traced.

I tucked the money into the waistband of my pants all around me, tightened my belt and buttoned my jacket. I heard the crunch of paper when I walked, but my own shuffle and the thud of the cane masked it.

Then I made the slow trek to the bus stop. I boarded the #17 with a group of tired workers in overalls and lunchboxes.

No one talked about the robbery during the bus ride. I was disappointed. This was the biggest thing to hit Albany in years, and it wasn't on everyone's radar.

I almost missed my stop. The driver sighed his impatience as I took a small eternity with my cane. The bus hissed in disgust and left me behind.

I was disoriented, but I soon spotted the sleeping-Mexican motel sign and made for the parking lot. I walked to Artie and Owen's room and knocked on the door.

I heard shifting sounds inside, a cough and then: "Who is it?"

"Charlie. Come on."

Something metallic fell to the floor and rolled away. I heard the drone of the TV inside. The door eased open. Artie's nervous face— a sliver of it—peeked out. His eye looked around me and he relaxed.

"Get in here." Artie ushered me in and slammed the door. He locked it. Owen sat on the edge of the bed. He had a band-aid on his forehead, over his right eyebrow.

"What happened?" We said this in unison. Artie waited for me to speak; I waited for him. "Is the camera okay? Did you get some good stuff?"

"I . . . think so." Artie sat in one of the uncomfortable chairs provided us by the Pay-Day Motel. "We kinda had to . . . leave it."

I felt my heart stop. "Where did you *leave* it?"

Neither said a word. Both studied their shoes. "*Where* did you leave it?"

Owen spoke. "Trash can. In the alley."

"Be more specific."

"By the movie theater."

"I need you to go get the equipment. All of it. Now."

"Now?"

"*Now.*"

Artie looked up at me. "There were police cars. I couldn't run with the suitcase."

"Why would you *want* to run?"

"Well . . ." Artie looked back at his loafers. "The police went into the theater. Like, two minutes after Sam got there."

"What happened?"

"Um. We didn't, uh, stick around to see."

"Okay. Fine. Now go to the bus stop. Get the equipment. *If* it's still there. And call me once you get it."

"Aren't you coming?"

I tried to remove my shoe. My foot was so swollen it wouldn't come up. "I gotta get this off."

"Get on the bed." Owen helped me up. I laid back.

"Do it."

"It might hurt."

"I don't care."

It hurt. I teared up and my nose ran. Artie pulled it off with such force it hit the far wall by the TV.

"Sorry, Charlie."

"Get the sock off."

"Oh, boy." Artie peeled it off an inch at a time. Blood stuck to the fabric; it'd soaked through my sock. The foot looked like something alien to my body. It was purple mottled with red and swollen beyond recognizable form.

"I guess this is your room now."

"Go get the equipment."

"Sorry, Charlie," Owen said.

"You did what you had to do. We don't want to lose a great scene. It might be the highlight of the picture. So: go. Leave the door unlocked and get back quick."

Through the picture window, I saw Artie and Owen in the middle of a hot discussion, with enough body language to tell the story. It would have played great for Laurel and Hardy.

The TV nattered in the background. Some local discussion show; through the poor reception it was hard to hear the conversation.

A bus came five minutes after they crossed to the stop. When it left, they were gone. Nothing to do but wait.

After a while, I leaned back on my elbows and looked at my foot. Swollen and discolored, it was still sticky with blood. It needed to be washed and dressed, but I knew I wouldn't make it off that bed.

I fell asleep; my body was spent. It wasn't dark when I woke. I hoped the boys had gotten the equipment. I looked at the foot. The swelling had gone down, and it didn't look so violent. I needed to clean the wound. That meant getting off the bed and across the floor to the bathroom. Millions of people did this every day. Even I could do it, with luck.

There's some footage missing in my memory. I found myself seated on the commode, my bad foot crossed over my good one. I remember the Winston cigarettes jingle from the TV. I was within reach of the sink, a clean washrag and towel and the little bar of pink soap they always leave. The first job was to pull the gauze off. I took it off like Artie had removed my sock: slow and measured. It hurt here and there, but I got it away from the wound.

I rinsed the wound area clean with warm water, soap and a washcloth that turned pink. When I had it clean, I wrapped it in toilet tissue. Then I put a bath towel around it—made a turban of the material.

Another jump cut: I got into bed and built up a pillow-and-blanket platform to elevate my foot. It hurt much less propped up. I lay flat on the bed and tried to relax. I didn't feel great about how this film was going. I didn't feel great about my foot.

I wondered where Sam was—if he was behind bars or hiding from the cops. He was a tough customer, and could take care of himself, but this was possibly the biggest event of his crime career, and I didn't want to have one of the stars of *Summer and Sandy* doing time when the film came out.

We still had some studio shots to finish on *Sandy*. I itemized them in my thoughts, remembered the storyboards Artie and I had done, and dozed off. The phone jarred me from a deep sleep. It wouldn't stop ringing, and I crawled to the nightstand and grabbed the receiver. My foot throbbed with a dull pain.

"Charlie. We got it."

"*Them*," Artie corrected.

"Yeah, *them*, and they're okay. We're going to the bus stop now."

"We stopped and had lunch."

"Everything's all right."

"Any sign of Sam? Or Charlotte?"

"No."

"I want you to go in the theater. See if either of them is still there. Will you do that now and call me right back?"

Owen sighed. "Okay."

"Hang up and buy a ticket."

"He said . . ." Owen hung up. I sighed and laid back. An announcer's voice brought on the Afternoon Movie—something called *Bullet Scars*, starring a young-looking Howard da Silva. It was talky and fast-paced, and its constant jabber soothed me back into nap mode.

Door knocks startled me awake. *Bullet Scars* was over; I was bathed in sweat. My teeth chattered; I couldn't control them. My whole body shook. "Come in," I shouted.

No reaction.

"*COME. IN.*"

"*Shut. Up,*" the voices from the wall replied. The door bumbled open. Artie and Owen showed the salvaged equipment.

Their smiles turned to horror as they got a good look at me. "Charlie! What the hell?"

"I need your help." My body and clothes were bathed in sweat. I got my room key from my pocket. "Please. Go get my stuff. The bandages and ointment. I need this foot cleaned up."

"Is that *okay?*" Owen pointed to my foot-turban. If it was bleeding, it hadn't soaked through the towel, but it throbbed, throbbed, throbbed, with the same thud in my temples.

"That is *not* okay." Artie got on the phone. "Hey. We need an ambulance . . . Room Eight. *Huh?* . . . No, not like that. Just call us an ambulance . . . *yes*. It's an emergency."

Without whacking my foot, and in the spirit of true friendship, Artie and Owen undressed me, brought me towels, helped me dry off, and gave me one of the thick terrycloth robes from the bathroom. It felt a million times better to be dry. I still had the chills.

"We gotta get you off that bed. Can you make it to the big chair?" With help from Artie and Owen, and the umbrella-cane, the answer was *yes*. I flopped down into the chair and Artie covered me with blankets.

"Glad the equipment was okay. Thanks for going and getting it."

"I'm excited to see the footage. But it can wait 'til you're better."

I couldn't decide whether to faint or sweat. I fainted.

FOURTEEN

I missed the ambulance arrival, the sirens, the rush down the highway and the admission to the hospital in downtown Albany. My movie resumed three days later with a wobbly POV shot from my hospital bed. Concerned doctors and nurses hovered around me. Artie, pale and stubbled, leaned against a wall. Owen slept sitting in a plastic chair, head hung down.

"*Back in the sad-dle again,*" I sang. It startled the nurse. "I'm awake. How about you?"

"Mister *Jerome?*" The doctor had a nasal voice that sounded sarcastic.

I moved my left foot. It was there. I tried to move my right foot. It wasn't there. "What the *hell?*"

"The operation went well. We had to remove your foot. You had a staph infection and it, ah. It appeared gangrene had set in. We don't get cases like this, but we . . . we didn't want it to spread."

"What about antibiotics? Penicillin? This isn't the Middle Ages."

"We tried that two days ago. The problem was . . . your fever. It wouldn't break. If we'd gotten that under control . . ." The doctor removed his glasses and closed his eyes. "We tried everything we knew. You have to understand. We're not a big hospital. We don't have the equipment—"

"Artie. What day is it?"

"Saturday."

I held my tongue; the f-word and s-word were ready to pop out.

"Who *okayed* this?" I gestured to my missing foot.

"They . . . they said it had to be done," Artie mumbled. "They didn't want to do it. You were out of your mind, Charlie. You kept opening the wounds up."

"You're lucky you get to keep most of your leg," the doctor said. "We terminated the infection."

I wanted to say: "What the *hell?!*" again, but what was the point?

"That's good," I sighed.

The doctor smiled. "They're doing wonders with prosthetics these days. You'll be up and walking in no time. They're really quite comfortable . . ."

"What the hell?" I thrashed my arms around me, as if that would brush away the bad dream and wake me up. I smacked a nurse hard in the face. The doctor called for backup and they gave me a shot. I faded out.

The camera fired up again. With some effort, I pried my eyelids open. Artie and Owen ate candy from a giant Whitman's Sampler. Owen looked guilty. Artie saw I was awake and tried to talk. "Chrmie." He cleared his throat and swallowed. "Nougats. Sorry about that."

Someone else was in the room—just out of my periphery. "Hay, man," Sam said. He arced around to my POV. "Good t' see yuh, Chorlie."

"You're alive."

"Yup."

"You're not in jail."

"Nope."

"Is Charlotte . . ."

"Mister Jerome, she's . . ." A toilet's flush told the story. Charlotte emerged from the bathroom, with its sign forbidding visitors to use the facilities. She looked like a million bucks in a fresh spring-colored dress.

"Our director." She curtsied. That made me laugh.

"Good to see you. So . . . I have so many questions." My stomach interrupted me. "Jesus, I'm hungry."

"Some candy?"

"Not right now. Can you call a nurse?"

Sam called for a nurse and I asked for ham and eggs, toast, coffee, and a glass of orange juice. The nurse smiled and exited the room.

No one had eaten the messenger boy piece, I so went for that. I bit off little slivers and dissolved them in my mouth. "So. What day is this?"

"The 13th."

"What day was the, uh, film shoot?"

"The 7th."

"*Wow.*" I turned to Sam. "So how did it go? What *happened*?"

Sam scoffed. "Nuthin'. I sat through that dang Western three times. Cops came in the thee-ater, but they didn' even try. They sat down an' watched the pitcher. I wawked right past 'em out the exit."

Sam's hardest task was getting Charlotte out of the bank. "I fixed my hair an' wawked back in there. That guard wouldn't stop tawkin' to 'er. I tole him Charlotte was my wife, an' he better stop payin' her so much attention. He looked at me like he c'd kill me when we left."

My jaw dropped as Sam talked. For a moment, I forgot about my foot and laughed hard. "You didn't get the papers, did you?"

"Been saving them for you." Charlotte dropped three folded newspapers in my lap. If laughter is the best medicine, I got a booster shot that lasted 'til my food arrived. The reportage of the robbery was like *The Onion* before *The Onion*. The bank staff, from the manager to the custodian, were a pompous, clueless lot. The bank hadn't been robbed since 1911, and though precautions to beef up security were mentioned, the article was an open invitation to rob the place again.

In the last of the three *Democrat-Herald*s, the police admitted they were stumped. All leads were cold. The "mystery woman" who granted the paper an extensive interview offered a cargo hold of red herrings—all taken as gospel by the local cops. "Fifty years ago, they hanged the bank robbers. Today, they got us back," said police chief Harvey Barnes.

My food arrived and I tucked into it. Sam and Charlotte made some noise about taking off. "Oh, Charlie. Someone from United Artists tried to call you this morning. They left a number. Where did I . . ." She rifled her purse, Sam's pockets and any other surface in her reach.

"Hrr," Artie said, caramel on his palate. He'd written the number on the lining paper of the Sampler. Calvin Cox at United Artists had found me at this rural hospital. I didn't recognize the name, but it must be important if he went to such trouble.

I troubled the nurse for a coffee refill. When she returned I asked if I could make a long-distance call. "It'll have to go on your bill."

"Fine. I'll pay. Is that okay?"

"Of course." I got an outside line, then an operator. Three minutes later, Calvin Cox answered. "Oh," he said when I identified myself. "We've had a hell of a time tracking you down."

"Did you get all the film elements?"

"Yes. They're here waiting for you. You still have some pickup shots—backlot stuff. We'd like it if you and the cast could get back here soon."

"I'm in the hospital right now." I told the story (minus *Never Odd or Even*) and he responded with "geez," "holy cow" and "yikes."

When I mentioned the fitting for the fake foot, Calvin Cox stopped me cold. "You get out of there as soon as possible. Come to Los Angeles for that. We have good hospitals here."

"I don't know how I'm going to pay for the prosthetic . . ."

"You're covered under union insurance. It happened during filming, right?"

"Uh? Yes. While we were filming." I cleared my throat. "Well, I'll see when I can get discharged. I'll probably be here a few more days."

"Can we send you anything?"

"I could use a good, stiff drink and something to read."

Calvin laughed. "Well, we found a first novel that we think you might be able to make a hell of a movie from. Give it a look-see; maybe it'll be a good fit for you."

We exchanged bland pleasantries and I ended the call. Artie and Owen were absorbed in a game show.

"Hey, guys. That was the guy from UA. They want us back in Hollywood. Soon as possible. I'll get my new foot in LA."

"Uh huh." They were hooked. The contestant was up to $14,000 and sweated out a crucial question. He blew it.

"*Aw*; too bad," Artie and Owen said over each other. Their interest in the contestant was over. "So. Back to Hollywood. When?"

I pressed the call button on the side of my bed. After a small eternity, an unfamiliar nurse showed up. "Sorry, hon, it's shift change. You need to use the restroom?"

"I'd like to see my doctor."

"Who's your doctor?"

"I don't know his name." I described him—a weary, bleary physician, steel-grey at the temples and careworn.

He reminded me of the actor Jay C. Flippen, but it was no good throwing that in. A scream and clattering metal broke our conversation. "No, you're *not*! You're *not* . . ."

A hairy, overweight man in an ill-fitting hospital gown padded down the hall. He ran into other people and waved his arms in horror. Orderlies pinned him to the floor and made him promise to be good. "I can't *stand* a thermometer there," the man said. "You *know* how it is."

Quiet returned to the ward. The nurse came back half an hour later. "Dr. Calkins is gone for the day. You can see him first thing in the morning. Oh. We need to clean and dress your, uh . . ." She gestured to where my right foot once was. "I'll get someone in here to take care of that."

"Do you have today's paper? Some magazines? Anything to read?"

"Okay, hon, we'll get you something."

The newspapers shielded me from the sight of whatever they did to my stump. It tingled and hurt a little, but it felt better when they had it freshly bandaged.

That morning's *Democrat-Herald* featured a police artist's sketch of the bank robber. He had horn-rim glasses, blond hair and a Van Dyke beard. The artist didn't get the cast of the eyes right, so he looked cross-eyed. Public enemy number one! It felt like the local cops were playing dumb so the robber(s) would be lulled into complacency and give themselves away.

Nah; that was giving these yokels too much credit. Soon it was dinner time (chicken parmesan with garlic toast and canned peas). Artie and Owen announced their departure as dinner arrived. Fine with me; my small talk skills were tanked out.

I ate and watched fuzzy nighttime dramas. At 10, a nurse brought me something to make me sleep. I slept.

"Excuse me, Mister Jerome." *The nurse was out of focus and at* an odd angle. "Telephone call from a Mr. Cox."

"What time izzit?" I wiped my eyes.

"10:25."

I yawned and cleared my throat. The nurse had the phone waiting. "Jerome here."

"*Charlie*! How'd you *sleep*?"

"Like a bag of rocks, Mr. Cox."

"Ha ha! It's *Calvin*, kid. Listen. I've spoken with the hospital, and the union is going to take care of your bill. What *we* need is for you to get back here so we can finish this picture. We should have a plane at the Albany airport first thing in the morning. Got to get you back on your feet." Calvin thought a moment about the deeper meaning of that stock phrase. "No pun intended."

"None taken. So . . . this will be for all of us?"

"You'll need your DP and Miss Magill. She's got a whole day of scenes with Irene Ryan and a couple of pickup actors. Simple stuff on the backlot."

Since he'd mentioned the foot, he told me they had a specialist lined up to fit me for a prosthetic device. "Goes right in your shoe. No one will ever know it's not real."

"Will I be able to walk?"

"I don't see why not. *I'm* no doctor, but they seem to know what they're doing." Cox cupped the phone and burst into a rant at some minion. "Heh heh. *Sorry* 'bout that. These student interns . . ."

My marching orders were to sit tight and to get everyone in the crew together to tell them the news. "See you here in a day or two."

It didn't take long to spread the news. Artie and Owen came in right before noon. Artie had a family size tin of Wise Bar-B-Q potato chips. His fingers were deckled with the greasy red-orange flavoring. Owen had a smaller bag of sour cream and onion chips, and buyer's remorse clouded his face.

Charlotte and Sam dragged themselves in while I ate breakfast/lunch. In-between bites of eggs and bacon and sips of coffee, I explained that UA needed us all back in Hollywood to finish *Summer and Sandy*. "I guess this means *Never Odd or Even* is over. For now. I'd like to finish it, and once I've taken a look at our footage we can come back to it. But for now, *Sandy* needs our attention."

I mentioned the flight and the Albany Municipal Airport. Sam turned pale. "*Oh*, no. You ain't gittin me up in wunna *them* things. *Naw*, sir. I ain't no fuckin *bird*."

"Haven't you been in a plane before?"

"No. An I ain't gonna *start*. That's my wors' nightmare. You read about them things crashin' an' explodin' *all* the damn time. *You* can go in that thing, but *I'm* drivin'."

Which reminded me—we had two cars. One was mine. "Owen? Are *you* a good driver?"

Owen had his hand deep in his chip bag. "I *guess* so. Never had an *accident*."

"Would you mind driving my car back to LA? I'll pay you. You can make a caravan with Sam."

"Okay." Owen loaded his mouth with chip fragments.

"If Sam's driving, *I'm* going with him." Charlotte looked adamant.

"As your director, *I* say you're *flying*. Sam isn't in any of the scenes we need to shoot. *You* are."

"But . . ."

"The picture comes *first*. You have a shot at an Oscar nomination. Hell, we *all* do. This movie is going to be a big thing. Let's get it done."

I saw reason in Charlotte's eyes. She hugged Sam and, in full dramatic mode, sighed: "The things we must do for our art."

Dr. Calkins didn't like the news that I was leaving. "You'll need crutches. And you'll have to keep your right leg elevated. I'm not sure how air travel might affect it."

"I've got to get back to work. My union insurance will take care of me."

"I hope all this is worth your while. I would hate for your wound to rupture. I did a closed amputation, with the idea that you would be fitted with a device here. The foot is tolerating our treatment plan. I'm worried that if there's too much movement—"

"I'll be sitting down while I work. I can work from a wheelchair if that's the best thing for me." We had the inevitable what-do-you-do conversation. I always cringe when I tell people that I make movies. It seems to bring out the dumbest questions.

Dr. Calkins was intrigued but didn't take the bait. "I don't get to the movies too often. I did like that *Anatomy of a Murder*, a couple years back."

He understood that I was under pressure to get back to LA and finish my picture. "See your doctor there first thing. Don't overtire yourself and get plenty of good food. If the healing process is good, you could be on your feet again within six months.

"Some people have emotional trauma after the loss of a limb. Or partial loss. Be sure to get help for that if it should happen. You seem to be taking this very calmly, Mister Jerome."

"It was a dumb accident." I shrugged. "You never see those coming. Crying over it seems useless to me."

Dr. Calkins nodded. A nurse interrupted him. Another patient had a bigger problem than mine.

In the margin of that morning's paper (which had bupkis on the bank robbery) I made a list of what needed to go on the plane and what could go in my car. I didn't want to entrust anything important or irreplaceable with Sam. I wasn't 100% sure he'd show up in LA as planned. Owen's tagalong presence might guilt him into doing the right thing. Maybe.

All the *Never Odd or Even* material—negatives, soundtrack, rushes and equipment—would go with Owen. I didn't want United Artists to know about this project. At this point, that film felt like a pipe dream. If *Summer and Sandy* became a hit—and I felt it would—the release of *Never* would be commercial suicide. Certainly, for Charlotte's career. I wasn't sure if Sam cared to continue as an actor. He had natural talent, and the camera loved him. But acting wasn't in his blood like it was with Charlotte.

Charlotte was, and is, a ham. You've seen her in *Murder, She Wrote* episodes, in commercials, in Hallmark Channel original movies (and I use that term loosely). She's been in everything— great films and stage plays, forgettable filler and annoyances. She lives to exist on-stage or on-screen in a persona. That's her essence.

But I digress. In a second column I wrote:

$$$ ALBANY

What to do with the loot from the robberies? We'd spent the proceeds from the savings and loan heist on film stock and camera equipment. I couldn't have a moral objection to the other money without being a hypocrite. But I really didn't want it around. None of us could spend those new bills. Those had to be on some federal watch list.

After much thought, I wrote: *with Sam.* He did the crime; his were the spoils. If he never showed up again, I'm sure he could figure an angle to get rid of the money or trade it for clean bills. I wanted no part of it.

The small amount of *Summer and Sandy* material would go with us on the plane. Artie and I would need to lay hands on that once we were home. We'd soon be deep in the editing process. Nothing else would matter for the duration.

I called everyone together one last time and gave them the final picture. A chartered prop plane would be ready for us at the Albany airport the next morning. The cabin seated six; I explained about my needing to elevate my right leg.

Owen was excited to be the keeper of the *Never Odd or Even* elements. And no one voiced offense at my decision to trust the money to Sam. I think none of us wanted it in our hands. What had happened was done, and we had it on film. "As for *Never Odd or Even.* I don't know if it will ever be finished. Maybe sometime down the road we can get back to it. Maybe it was just an experiment I had to get out of my system." I paused at the next thought. "Maybe it was just a dumb idea. My biggest fear is that I've wasted your time with it."

"Of *course* not," Artie said as he cut off Charlotte. "I learned a lot from it. And we might have some—"

"It was worth it all just for my time with Clarence," Charlotte interrupted. "And it all stays between us. Agreed?"

All parties murmured in assent. "*I* wood'n mind workin' on it s'more," Sam said. "But I *git* it. We don' talk about it."

"I'll be discharged at 10 tomorrow morning. Artie, you help Owen get all the film stuff stowed away in my trunk. You and Charlotte be here in the morning. Sam, you can take off whenever. I'd like you and Owen to leave at the same time. And stay together. It's important."

Both nodded. The door swung open. A nurse wheeled in a shiny metal cart. It was time to change my dressing.

Sam and Owen hit the road that afternoon. Owen surprised me. He bought two copies of a gas station map and highlighted the route in red pen on both. He gave one to Sam after he went over the trip with him. "We have about 900 miles to cover, and, um, it gets real foggy once you cross over into California. So let's do it in two, uh. Chunks."

Owen had a planned stopover in Eureka, California. "If we get going after 10 in the morning, we'll beat the fog and we can, uh, go the rest of the way. In a day."

"As you *wish*," Sam replied with sarcasm. I wanted to sock him. Owen thought out a good plan. I don't think the kid could have tied his own shoes before he got onto my film crew.

"Sam, you be good to Owen. Look at what he's *done*. He's put some time and *thought* into this. And it's to make sure you *both* get back safely. Right? *Safely*."

"Yeah, safely." Sam took his map and tucked it in his blazer pocket. "Well . . . Charlotte mus' be runnin' late. She was s'pose'ta see me off."

As if on cue, Charlotte appeared, in the dress she wore when she seduced Clarence. "They tried to tack on all these false charges at the motel. I read them the riot act!"

She embraced Sam and they kissed. "'Mine *me* t' read you th' riot act sometimes." He smiled and took her hand for moment. "See you back *home*. *Co*-star."

"Not before I see *you*. *Co*-star." One more smooch and Sam and Owen were gone. I felt the way a parent must feel when their child goes off to college/war/travel. Owen held all the *Never Odd or Even* material for the next two days. I hoped he was a careful driver. I didn't want him to get hurt; I sure as hell didn't want those film elements to have any trouble.

Artie showed up at six with a surprise: takeout Chinese. "You need a break from that hospital grub." He'd gotten plenty for the three of us. Charlotte scared up a card table and set it up to the right side of my bed.

"Thanks, Artie. Thanks to *all* of you. We've worked hard and you know *what*? We've made a damned *movie*! *Two* movies, but . . . we've done something a lot of people don't have a clue about. They just go to the theater and shove popcorn in their faces and watch. Well, we're gonna give 'em something to watch. Something they'll think about and remember. How many people get to do that and make a living?"

Everyone nodded.

"Wish I had some champagne so I could make a toast to you. You've both got a big future. You'll look back on this as your first picture—the thing that launched you to something better."

"You too, Charlie." Artie toasted me with chopsticks and noodles.

"And here's to Barrett. He gave us all something to do."

"To Barrett," Charlotte and Artie slurred through mouthfuls of rice and chow mein.

"We should call him," Charlotte said after she swallowed. "Let him know we're coming back."

"Sure. Soon as we eat."

We ate. And ate. We got to the fortune cookies. I opened mine and read it out loud:

> YOUR AMBTIONS WILL COME TRUE
> IN REWARD FOR YOUR HAD WORK

Typos aside, it was a good omen. Charlotte's said:

> YOU WILL BE LUCKY IN LOVE AND CAREER

Blunt but promising. Artie's read:

> HE WHO RISES EARLY GETS LIFES RICH REWARDS

They dropped an extra fortune cookie in the bag. I didn't want to jinx our good mood. I wadded the bag, crushed the wrapped cookie and tossed it all on the table. "That hit the spot. Thanks,

Artie."

"It was surprisingly good for . . . for where we are."

"Hicksville."

"Goober City."

"Doofus Holler."

A nurse ended our festivities. She reminded me that there would be an ambulance to drive me to the municipal airport at 10 AM, and that I'd need to get up around 7 to get ready for the flight. They had to wrap up my right leg so that the stump wouldn't be impacted by all the movement and the changes in air pressure.

It was half past seven; I begged for another hour with my friends. "We need you asleep by 10. I'll be back with your meds at 9:30."

Artie scared up a deck of cards. Since we had a card table, why not? Artie and Charlotte slaughtered me over several hands of five-card rummy. I'd get part of a good run, then the cards turned their back on me. I held onto two aces, in the hope of getting a third, which showed up on my last draw. I laid those three cards down; Artie held the remaining ace and went out on us. I came out ahead on that hand and decided to quit while I was still among the living.

During the hands, we talked about Sam and Owen, and wondered how they were doing on their drive.

"Oh, shoot. We forgot about Barrett." Charlotte looked at her cards with disgust.

"Do you know his number?" I asked Artie.

"Does he have a phone?"

"I can't remember. Well, we'll get him tomorrow. He's probably been worried sick about us."

"He's a worrier," Artie agreed. "Eight on your nine and I'm out."

The ambulance ride was quick. I sat in a wheelchair with my right leg extended. The wheelchair skidded around in the back of the vehicle until I got the brakes locked. I'm lucky I didn't break the damned leg.

The plane was warmed up and ready to take off. With Artie's help, I hopped up the rickety portable stairwell and into the back seat, which was one continuous cushion. I asked for a couple of pillows and I laid down. Artie and Charlotte sat on opposite sides of the aisle.

Charlotte discovered a manila envelope with my name on it. Inside was a short note from Calvin Cox and a copy of a thin novel by Harold N. Jackson, *No Room at The Royal*. The plane readied for blast-off as I read the copy on the dust jacket:

A true-to-life account of a young salesman who can't find a hotel room in New York City. Forced to spend the night on his feet, Dana Altheimer sees a side of the city unknown to those who inhabit it by day. His experiences change the way he looks at life and will amuse, terrify and surprise you as you walk the dark streets with him, sales case in hand . . .

The captain murmured something about seat belts and the engines revved into high gear. I found one near my waist and cinched it up. No point in me rolling up and down the aisles.

The motors were too loud to allow conversation, so I read. *No Room at The Royal* was a great little book. The urban setting and its episodic structure would make a damned good picture. I'd transplant it to Los Angeles, since the downtown area and Bunker Hill had a motherlode of run-down locations that the camera loved to death. And the story would allow me to go off-script and have interactions with real denizens of the streets. I could get a little realism into the story. If I could work some of that Okie accent off Sam, he might be a good fit for Dana Altheimer, the main character. We'd have to change that name. It sounded too made-up.

As I finished the book, I felt like I'd been handed a gift. I could make this on a low budget, and with Artie as DP, those ragged locations would look like a million bucks. I'd write the script for this. No sense letting other hands touch it. *No Room at The Royal* would be closer to the truthful fiction I wanted my movies to be. The title was great, too. It'd look good on a marquee.

The co-pilot brought us some coffee and checked in on me. He said there'd be a car waiting to take me to a hospital—to check on my right leg and make sure nothing had gone wrong. I wasn't in any pain. The leg tingled, but air travel hadn't aggravated it.

We had a lull in the noise, and I called out to Artie. I showed him the book. "This is gonna be our next picture. Read it. It's really good." Artie showed the book to Charlotte. There wasn't a role for her, but I'd invent one—a young girl who's in the same predicament as the main character. Maybe she keeps popping up throughout the night, and the two get to know each other. There wouldn't be any romance. Instead, both would part with that sad feeling that there *could've* been something, if only the time was right.

Yes, that would end the movie on a beautiful note. Morning, the city coming to life, and these two tired people going their separate ways, haunted by the events of the night, knowing they could never relive them, never recapture them . . .

The plane made a clumsy landing. We got jostled and the book slid to the front of the cabin. After the plane taxied to a stop, Artie tried to fetch the book. The pilot's door popped open and knocked it back down the aisle to me. I handed it to Artie. "Hang onto it— we're gonna need it!"

An ambulance rode me to a hospital. Calvin Cox, in horn-rim glasses and a three-button suit, waited there for me. "*Charlie!* Good to *see* you!"

I couldn't recall ever meeting him before. I shook his hand. "Likewise."

"So, what do you *think?*"

I thought for a moment. "The book. Terrific. I'm sold. It'll make a great movie. I have some ideas . . ."

While the LA doctors looked at the amputation spot and redressed it, I pitched my ideas for *No Room*—moving it to Los Angeles and introducing the girl character. Calvin nodded with great enthusiasm. "Wow! I can see it now. Brilliant! *Great!*" Calvin tried to sell me on working with a young Czech cinematographer, but I told him I wanted Artie as DP. "Once you see some of the footage on *Sandy,* you'll get it. Artie's a keeper."

"We can't wait to see some of the picture—when it's ready. Even a rough cut. This picture has built up a lot of anticipation. Warners and M-G-M are kicking themselves that they didn't get an option on it. *Kicking* themselves!" Calvin cackled with glee.

"There was no reason to amputate," my doctor said. "They didn't know what they were doing. We could have saved your foot, Mister Jerome."

He recited a narrative of how he and his staff would have treated the wounds. Major doses of antibiotics, since he felt I had cellulitis—the reason my fever wouldn't break for a few days—and the elevation of the leg above heart level to reduce stress and swelling. All fine and dandy, but the deed was done.

He said the surgery was well done. "If they'd taken as much care with your treatment, this wouldn't have happened."

"Well, nothing we can say or do will bring that foot back." I shrugged; what else could I do?

The doctor nodded.

The fitting for my prosthetic was scheduled for two days out. It wouldn't be difficult or traumatic. In the interim, they swathed the foot in bandages and padding and gave me crutches. I was advised not to spend a great deal of time in an upright position unless it was necessary. I told them I'd be sitting for my work. Taking a bath or shower in the tub would be impossible for the time being, but I could have a sponge bath whenever I wanted.

Charlotte and Artie waited in the lobby for me. I wanted to surprise them by coming to them on crutches. I almost fell a couple of times, but I got into the swinging rhythm of the walk. For a moment, the thought that I'd lost a foot got to me, but I crutched my way out of depression and tried to focus on the future. We'd get *Sandy* done, and it would be a success. Then we'd move on to *No Room at The Royal* . . .

Something wasn't right. Artie wasn't eating. He sat with his elbows on his thighs and stared at nothing. Charlotte daubed tears with a handkerchief and shook her head. Were they really that worried about me? I was fine, all things considered.

"I'm *fine!*" I called out. Neither heard me. I crutched closer, giving my lower body bigger swings. I got the image of the comedian Charley Chase, with his spry, beanpole body, and imagined this was how he'd look on crutches.

"Hey! I'm *okay!*" I was four feet from them. Artie started and looked at me like I was a ghost. Charlotte looked up with reddened eyes.

"Oh, Charlie. Oh, *Charlie* . . ." She teared up again.

"I'm going to be all right. Please don't worry . . ."

"It's not you. Not *you* . . ." She bowed down into her hanky. Artie focused his eyes. I eased into a chair across from them. I set my crutches on the floor. "Read it . . ." He handed me an afternoon paper.

This was the headline:

OREGON 'MYSTERY BANDIT' DEAD IN FIERY CRASH
Loot from Last Robbery Scattered Across California Highway; Body Identified as Career Criminal John Beemis

Shock jolted me as I read the first few paragraphs. "John Beemis" would take some getting used to; Sam Mellinger was one of many aliases this fellow had used in a 15-year string of small crimes.

The accident happened just before dawn, outside of Eureka, California. Apparently, Sam/John decided to get a head start on the last leg of the trip. Despite fog warnings, he took off on a highway course of hairpin turns and steep inclines.

He got about eight miles, driving at high speed through the fog and the road's unpredictable esses and zees. A dairy truck, stalled at an angle across the highway, was Sam's Waterloo.

The driver of the dairy truck, Bill Melson, was standing on the road shoulder and saw the whole thing. "This white car come out of the fog like it was in the Indy 500. Must have been doing 80. I don't think he had time to see the truck. I hit the ground right before he hit.

"The crash was awful, and then the engine blew up. I saw red and orange. And then there was this quiet. And I heard what sounded like a bunch of pigeons taking off. Only it was money. Bills, flapping in the air, going all over Christendom. I picked up one; it was a 100-dollar bill."

No mention of Owen; I wouldn't imagine him to step up and connect himself with Sam. The serial numbers of the bills matched a list that the Albany police department had circulated. What was left of Sam made for a hard ID, but he'd been jailed and fingerprinted once, and enough of his prints remained to be proof positive that it was John Beemis. The co-star of *Summer and Sandy*, who we all knew as Sam Mellinger—which sounded like Dillinger, I realized.

I looked up from the paper. I'd forgotten where I was, and Artie's gaze surprised me. "Holy shit," I said. I shook my head, as if that would coax anything more profound from my mouth. It didn't.

"You haven't heard from Owen . . ." I said. Then I realized that was impossible. There's no way Owen could have known we were here at the hospital. "Let's go to my apartment. We've got a lot to deal with." I looked at Charlotte. "Charlotte, I'm so sorry. I don't know what else to say . . ."

Charlotte nodded and managed a smile. She tucked her handkerchief in her bag. I got to my feet and crutches and we hailed a cab outside the hospital.

We rode in stunned silence. I looked out at familiar buildings and streets, seeing them but not seeing them. My thoughts went from pragmatic—*thank goodness all of Sam's scenes were covered*—to heartbroken. I liked Sam, and it was a privilege to give him an outlet as an actor. He was used to pretending he was someone else, but the role of Sandy gave him a positive focus for all the tricks he'd picked up along the road of life.

The guy had talent and promise. He had a future in movies—if that's what he truly wanted. And in Charlotte, he had a co-star, and maybe a wife and partner. The kid had it made. Everything right in his pocket. And then everything was kaput. I hoped I had something to drink. This was a time to get drunk and ponder the unfathomable.

FIFTEEN

I had a full bottle of bourbon. I found it after I got the lights on. Artie and Charlotte found the couch and I brought glasses, booze and ice to them.

I poured three glasses and handed them out. "To Sam," I said as a toast. "Or *John*. Whoever he was, he didn't have *this* coming."

"He was a kind soul," Charlotte added. "He didn't want to hurt *anyone*. I *loved* him . . ."

"The *camera* loved him." Artie's hand shook. "Jeezus, he didn't even have a *chance*. Just one picture. But it's one hell of a *good* picture."

"And we're going to finish it for Sam's sake. *Prost*."

We drank. Artie coughed. Coffee was more his speed. I cleared my throat and adjusted my giant foot on its coffee table perch. "So. What do we *do* here? Do I tell United Artists about . . . *this*?" I gestured to the newspaper on the coffee table. "Or do we create a legend? Does Sam Mellinger fade out of sight?"

"We have the what's-his-name angle . . ." Artie thought. "*Dean*. James *Dean*. With the accident and all . . ."

"But then Sam's remembered as a criminal who just happened to make a movie. I don't think that's how he wanted to go." I looked at Charlotte. "You got to know him . . . really well. What do *you* think?"

Charlotte sipped her bourbon. "What do *I* think?" She looked in her purse for something. She didn't find it. "I vote for the *legend*. Sam Mellinger, who came out of nowhere and made just this one movie. And then, no more . . . *no more* . . ."

Charlotte had a lot of crying to do, and Artie and I sat and let her go. We wanted to talk, but respectful silence seemed like the right atmosphere.

The phone rang. It was like a kick in the teeth.

"M-Mister J—Charlie." Owen sounded like a motherless child.

"Where are you?"

"Um. Home. I came by a couple of hours ago. I'm okay. And the stuff is okay."

"Stuff. Stuff?"

"The . . . the *movie* stuff."

"Oh." I'd forgotten about *Never Odd or Even*.

"Are . . . are *you* okay?"

"We're sitting here trying to swallow the bad news."

"I . . . *I* should come over. I have some news you ought to know."

"Come over. And bring the stuff."

"Owen," I said to my fellow mourners. "He's coming over to join the wake." Charlotte nodded through her tears. Artie looked tense and twiddled his thumbs. "I'll call Barrett in the morning. He might make Owen a little uncomfortable."

Owen's diffident knock sounded 20 minutes later. He was dressed like the son of a well-off film executive—monogrammed short-sleeve sports shirt and tan slacks with deck shoes and his hair combed neatly. "The, um, stuff's in your car."

"My car's okay?"

"Yeah. Fine."

"Well." Owen slid past me and went into the living room.

"Artie. Miss Magill."

"Oh, call me *Charlotte*. There are no formalities here."

"I'm really *sorry* about what happened. I *tried* to talk him out of it." Owen had the floor. He cleared his throat.

"Sam was . . . I mean, I didn't know him too well, but he was . . . acting *strange*. When we left, at first, I was the leader. I w-worked out a system with him. Like, if I had to stop for gas, or to, uh, pee, I reached up and patted the top of the car twice.

"That was okay for the first couple of hours. We stopped at a gas station. I had to go real bad. And after I washed my hands and got a Coke from the machine, Sam was gone. Like, vanished. I drove for two hours before I caught up with him. He had someone else in the car with him."

"*Who?*" Charlotte almost stood up.

"*Wait*, wait. It was some *guy*. *Older* guy. He looked like someone Sam knew. They talked a lot. I could see the older guy doing, you know . . ." Sam made hand gestures as some people do when they talk.

"So now *Sam* was the leader. He stuck to the map. It was starting to get dark, and we turned a bend and came on this town. There was a big diner off the highway. Sam did the roof thing and I knew he wanted to go there. So, I followed.

"It was some big gaudy truck stop—Sam's kind of cuisine. It sounded like it had a honky-tonk attached to it. I felt a little scared goin' in there. There were some rough customers in that place."

Sam introduced Owen to his friend, Gray. "I think that was his name. I couldn't hear too good. I guess he and Sam had been in *jail* together? That's what it sounded like. Anyway, they were old friends. They talked about . . . well, they'd done a bunch of stick-ups together.

"Sam told him all about the job in Albany. He didn't say anything about being in the *movies*. It was like he didn't want his friend to know about *that* at *all*. He made out like he'd just been doing stick-ups the whole time. He said this was the best one he'd ever done."

"Would you like a *drink*?" Artie interrupted, as was his wont.

"S-sure." Artie poured a short neat bourbon and handed it to Owen.

"Whoa, that's *strong*!" Owen took a considerable sip and continued. "So . . . Sam showed this Gray fellow . . . maybe it was Ray? It doesn't matter. So he showed this guy some of the money from the robbery. Some of the new bills. He broke open a bundle and these two guys fingered and smelled the bills. It was kind of creepy.

"We had pot roast and baked beans and apple pie with ice cream. I had coffee. They had beer. Sam got pretty stewed. And then when they brought the bill, Sam slapped down one of those 50-dollar bills on the table. The lady stared at it, like she didn't know what to do with it. We took off as soon as she walked away. Sam was laughing like he'd pulled the best joke ever."

"'See yuh in Yoo-reeka,' Sam said. He and this guy got in the car and took off like a streak down the highway. Right after that, the waitress came out into the parking lot with a couple of police. I ducked down in the seat 'til the coast was clear. And then I drove under the speed limit all the way to the state border. I didn't want anyone to take a second look at me."

Owen finished his bourbon. "Oh *boy*, that's strong."

"So, you got to California . . ." I was anxious to hear the rest.

"Oh *yeah*." Owen was now a little drunk. "So, I, uh, I got to California and I found this motor inn where we were s'posta spend the night. I pulled in the lot and I didn't see Sam's car. I went to the office and checked in. I asked did the desk guy see Sam or his buddy. He said no. But he said there was a bar about a half mile down the road. That was the next closest place to the motor inn.

"I drove there and sure enough, Sam's car was there. There was country music playing—live music, and it was *loud*. You couldn't hear yourself *think*. I spotted them at a table.

"Now, I'm not this guy's *mom*, or anything. I couldn't *make* him stop drinking. I told him I was checked into the motel, and that he should check in and sleep it off. 'Cos we had another long drive in the morning."

Owen kept a vigil until three AM. No sign of Sam. He got worried. "I drove back to where that bar was. The lot was empty. Nobody. The highway was, like, dead. Fog was coming in. It was kind of scary. So, what could I do? I went back to my room and went to sleep.

"I woke up about 10. I didn't mean to sleep so late. I guess I was worn out. I took a shower and went up to pay for my room. I asked the lady at the desk if Sam had ever checked in. She said she didn't see anyone that fit the description. I looked at the sign-in log but all I saw after my name was a couple of Mr. and Mrs. signatures. So. I started out towards here. I kept hoping I'd see Sam's car. I stopped at a little market to get some stuff to eat in the car. They had sandwiches and chips.

"Right about noon, I came across the wreck. They had the Highway Patrol flagging down people. There was one lane of highway that you could still drive on, and they let one car at a time, from each direction, go through.

"I recognized Sam's car—what was *left* of it. It was all scrunched up. Scorched real bad in the front part. I guess they'd taken Sam away—what was left of *him*. They were still going after the money. Those bills had gotten all over the shoulder of the road, and in this gully."

Sam cleared his throat. "I would of called you right then, but I didn't know how to reach you. I got back here like two hours ago. I was expecting Dad to be all angry at me. But he said how much you appreciated me, and what a good job I did. That made him kinda like me. He said he was proud of me. He got me this."

Owen pulled a deluxe Swiss Army knife out of his pocket. That must have been Dad's go-to gift. I was off the hook. I'd have to get Owen something else to show my appreciation for his doing a good job and being a good kid.

"Well. I guess that's about it. I sure am sorry he's gone. How are you going to finish the movie, Mist—*Charlie*?"

"All of Sam's scenes were filmed. And I have some wild footage that I can still work into the movie in editing. Some good reaction shots and insert stuff, if we need it."

"Oh. That's good. I meant, the *other* movie."

"The other movie. Speaking of which, how's about you and Artie go get that stuff."

Owen wouldn't have passed a breathalyzer test. He weaved as they walked outside in the late twilight to my car. It took them three trips; the developed film was heavy, and the other stuff was awkward to haul. Artie had to do the lifting; on their last trip, they brought in the suitcase-cam and the portable tape recorder.

For the time being, I stashed all the *Never Odd or Even* footage in my bedroom closet. I didn't know what to do with it. With Sam gone, it seemed pointless to go any further.

We all needed a good night's sleep. In the morning, Artie and I had a meeting with Calvin Cox and then we'd get to work on finishing *Summer and Sandy*. And I'd finally call Barrett, who must have been beside himself wondering whatever happened to his pet project.

SIXTEEN

I got my new right foot the next week. By that time, we'd shot the needed scenes for *Sandy*. I directed from a wheelchair.

Irene Ryan noticed the difference in Charlotte's ability as an actress. They worked together so well I reshot a couple of important scenes. They had chemistry, and they buzzed right through the retakes. I'm glad I had the opportunity to improve those parts of the film.

And just for the hell of it, I asked them to improvise a couple of short scenes. "I want the audience to feel like they know who you are," I told them. I gave them one-word topics: *adolescence, memories*. And off they ran. One of the best scenes in the movie came out of these spontaneous bits. It's that moment where Irene and Charlotte are sitting on the porch swing on a summer evening. Irene keeps saying that it's going to rain like the dickens. Charlotte asks Irene what her first time was like—in the innuendo movies used to get past the Production Code.

Irene's eyes light up and she tells about meeting a traveling salesman. He wasn't much older than she and didn't seem confident about his lot in life. He saw a sign for a village dance and asked her to go with him. "He wasn't much of a dancer," Irene recalls, embedded in her character. "But we didn't do much dancing that night."

They ended up in a barn, trapped by a sudden downpour—the trigger for her reminiscence.

She implied the consummation of this brief relationship. It was an awkward and new experience for them both. They stayed put until the salesman heard the whistle of an eastbound train. He had to move on.

"Never saw him again and didn't expect to. Thanks heavens, nothing came of it." She winked at Charlotte to say what words couldn't yet express on the movie screen. "But that got me thinking, just like you. That there was a bigger world out there—bigger than I had any idea of. It was up to me whether I got there. And I never quite made it. Always something held me to here. And I always *regretted* getting held to here. But it was my life, and I couldn't walk out on it."

I had a studio rainstorm ready on cue, and as that line ended, I gave the signal. Fake rain drummed down hard on the backlot. With it came startlingly good rumbles of thunder. "I *told* you we were in for it," Mrs. Ryan said. "I'll make some coffee." She shambled off-scene and I moved the camera in for a medium shot on Charlotte. In character, she was stunned by the story she'd just heard. Patterns of the rain reflected on her face. It was a great shot, and I let the camera stay on it as long as Charlotte needed.

That scene has gotten acclaim in essays, books and documentaries, and it's always attributed to Barrett Broadford. At first, he fended it off, saying it was something the actresses cooked up. But as time went by, it became part of the legend of the movie, and a key moment in his career. I let him have it. It was a fair trade for keeping him out of *Never Odd or Even.*

Charlotte and I invented the legend of Sam Mellinger. We wrote a letter to Charlotte, from Sam, saying that he enjoyed making the film, but he had to see Europe. If he liked Paris, he might settle down there. In the meantime, please see that whatever payment he had coming his way be given to Charlotte to send on to him. He didn't want his address known. "I need some time to think about my future. I hoep (sic) you understand."

I had a friend on the staff of the *International Herald-Tribune* in Paris. I sent the letter to him—an envelope within an envelope— and asked him to mail it back to the States. It was addressed to Charlotte; its return address was *somewhere in France.*

It took the letter two weeks to come back to us. In its travels, it was torn, bent and water-stained. It was a perfect artifact from abroad. No one would doubt it was the truth. Charlotte called her agent and channeled panic in an Oscar-worthy performance. He demanded she come to his office. I tagged along.

"These damned kids," Sam Schacks said as he read the letter.

"Well, this doesn't change a thing. The movie still goes out. If this kid wants to prance around Paris and write poetry . . . well, there ain't no law against it. Maybe he'll get this out of his system when he sees how this picture goes over." Sam looked up at us, his eyes bagged with dark, as if we had the answer to this letter. All I could do was shrug.

I expected Calvin Cox to have a fit. Instead, he was delighted. "This is a publicity dream! So romantic! Wait 'til I show this to Sol and Amanda. They'll spin this into gold!" He laughed so hard his horn-rims slipped off his nose.

The gossip columns and movie magazines ate the story up. It was Swoonville: dashing, handsome and gifted newcomer conquers cinema in his first (and only) film; forsakes the glitz of Hollywood for the purity of art in romantic, mysterious Paris. "If it sounds like a fairy tale," one prominent columnist said, "it's a reminder that, even in this big, bad world, fairy tales do occasionally come true."

It sounded like a fairy tale because it *was* one. But it made for good copy, good publicity and it insured interest in *Summer and Sandy* before it reached theaters.

The movie edited like a dream. Artie's cinematography was raw, real and soaked up the rainy atmosphere of Oregon in the location scenes. The soundstage stuff was never going to match the look and feel of those sequences, but he got a richness to the greys, a depth to the blacks and a slight overexposure of the whites—all which made cookie-cutter backlot scenes come to life. As a person, he's a goofball—he'll tell you that himself—but his eye reaches through the camera lens and brings depth and clarity to whatever he shoots.

We got in every frame of footage we had on Sam—except for out-takes and botched scenes. Barrett's screenplay had its sappy moments, but it was tight, and our first cut came to 99 minutes.

We ran that cut for a group of suits in United Artists' screening room. The picture got to them. It reminded them that they were once unformed, larval youth, eager for experience but unable to figure out how to find it. Thus, it found *them*, and often in painful, confusing ways.

Calvin Cox took me aside as the execs milled out. "It's beautiful, Charlie. Just . . . beautiful. It made me laugh; it made me tear up. This will kill at the box office. One small suggestion . . ."

That suggestion was to cut two minutes towards the middle of the picture. It was some character stuff that I really liked, but I heard Calvin out: it made a lull in the movie where it couldn't bear to slow down.

I heeded his advice and trimmed those two minutes. After an enthusiastic preview in Santa Monica, I lopped off another 90 seconds here and there. Now 95 minutes, *Summer and Sandy* was tight as a drumhead. Every moment counted.

I felt like we had a winner on our hands.

The Duane Eddy theme song was released as a single on Jamie Records. A month before the picture hit national screens, it got up into the Top 30. After *Sandy* was released, it went back in the charts and topped off at #18.

You know the rest of the story. The critics loved it; we got a couple of lukewarm notices from old farts who were better off retired. You're always going to get a bad review somewhere. College students loved the film; high schoolers saw it over and over. Mature audiences in search of one last moment of their youth went to it and loved it.

My first pro film turned a nice profit. I was in like Flynn, and pre-production was underway for *No Room at The Royal*. Barrett was hurt that I didn't ask him to write the screenplay, but I knew how this story worked, and I couldn't translate that to another person. I assured him that we'd work together again—maybe on the next picture.

I was halfway through the third draft of the screenplay when they announced the Oscar nominations. I wasn't surprised by Barrett's nom for Best Original Screenplay, but my getting the nod for Best Director floored me. I knew I didn't stand a chance to win—too many big names on that list, all established people who'd paid their dues. I imagined some resentment at a kid like me getting on the list, but it meant that enough Academy members really liked the film to cast their vote. Maybe it was a show of encouragement for young talent in Hollywood. I hadn't earned it; I didn't deserve it.

It was the only nod I ever got from the Hollywood system. Not that the Oscars mean much, in the long run. Few of the winning movies really stand the test of time. The Academy votes on zeitgeist, and on whose turn it is to get to stand in line and read their thank-yous and collect their statue—which winds up dusty on a display shelf or used as a paperweight on their desk at home.

And what of Barrett? He was fine back home. He'd gotten some gigs writing earnest, message-heavy hour-long TV dramas, and he sat in on some of the *Sandy* editing sessions. I ran him Irene Ryan's improvised bit about losing her virginity. I half expected him to be petulant about it, but he was wowed. "You *couldn't* sit down and write that. You just *couldn't*. Thank you, Charlie."

"Thank Irene next time you see her. I'm glad you liked it. Didn't want you to feel like I was horning in on your part of the picture."

By that time, she was working on *The Beverly Hillbillies*, and the world never saw that side of her again. I guess Granny paid the bills, but it was a criminal waste of her talent. I know I've said this before. It still bothers me. It's almost worse than her not getting any work at all. But it's part of history.

We kept the Mellinger myth alive. Over the next three years, with Charlotte's input, we sent letters to Paris to be mailed back by my friend. We kind of had to. Sam's performance and screen demeanor made a lot of teenage girls (and gay men) fall in love with him. The letters, which were relayed to the Hollywood gossip mill, kept the story going that Sam was alive and well and writing poetry in Paris.

A camera team for *Life* magazine went to Paris and wasted two weeks searching for Sam. They published a photo essay of "Sam's Paris"—crooked cobblestone streets, open-air cafes, rows of crumbling apartments—and hinted that a book of Mellinger poetry was due from a major publisher.

That was another goodie planted in one of the letters. Charlotte and I collaborated on a book of Sam's poems. Charlotte dictated ideas and I translated them into free verse—no metered rhymes for Sam!

They were little better than Rod McKuen's stuff, but Simon &

Shuster snapped up *Lines from My Life*, as we called it, in a cute little square-shaped hardcover that breezed through five printings in 1964.

Since Sam wasn't available for interviews, Charlotte and I faked an exclusive Q&A, credited to my friend at the *Herald-Tribune*—a piece that was syndicated globally. Sam had (and continues to have) a big following in Japan, and his poems were a huge hit there. And in Germany, France, Brazil and other countries.

The money from the book and Sam's screen work went into a trust for young actors, The Mellinger Foundation, which continues to this day. I hope it's helped some kid who had the ambition to enter the field of acting. It's no bed of roses.

Charlotte did the part of the girl in *No Room at The Royal*. Her character had some of Lisa's small-town innocence, but she brought a Shirley MacLaine kind of exuberance to the character. The male lead was an unknown named Wes Calder, and he was good in the role of Jack Anderson, as I renamed the character. He went into TV. You've seen him in shows like *The Rockford Files, The Night Stalker* and *Quincy*. He had a touch of the young Redford to him, but TV acting was Easy Street. Work was plentiful, and if an actor could accept working under stress and lesser conditions, he or she could get a lot of character roles. I don't blame any actor for taking that route.

Sam's last letter from France, dated July 1966, stated that he was moving to Africa to study wildlife and paint the landscapes of that continent.

He was never heard from again.

EPILOGUE

1

I've continued to be heard from—not much lately, but I've managed to make a film every couple of years. I've made the movies I wanted to make, within and without the studio system. The late 1970s and '80s, when the industry went to shit with kiddie adventure flicks and the birth of movie franchises, was hell for independent filmmakers. I wasn't about to direct a *Scooby-Doo* movie, or any of the other diarrhea Hollywood spurted out into the Porta-Potties that movie theaters became.

I had a brief resurgence in the 1990s, when younger indie filmmakers paid lip service to me in interviews. I think Quentin Tarantino said he liked the life in my movies. *No Room at The Royal* was allegedly one of his favorites—on a list that changed every half hour.

I didn't come back to *Never Odd or Even* until my slump in the late '70s. I put the film cans into dry storage in the late '60s, and the project haunted the edge of the movies I made before the merry go round broke down.

I did a couple of all-improvised features—*Goin' Down*, a 1969 comedy-drama about the generation gap and the tensions in American life, and *Thorns in the Bed of Roses*, a 1973 piece about disillusionment and alcoholism. Herschel Bernardi was great in the lead role of that picture as Zach, an ad exec whose drinking had worn him down and burned him out. It was an honor to work with him. He should have gotten an Oscar for his performance. I think the movie nailed its mood and subject matter so thoroughly that it made people uncomfortable. Along with *No Room at The Royal*, it's my favorite of the films I've been lucky enough to get made.

Never Odd or Even saved my bacon. In 1978, I was, shall we say, at liberty. Hollywood was on an extended break from thinking, and the kind of movies I made weren't box office any more. I'd saved enough to be able to coast for a few years, and I did a little TV work during that time, but my future looked cloudy. The world I'd known and worked for wasn't the same anymore.

This was my middle age crisis, about a decade too early. After one too many empty afternoons, I booked some time in an editing room after I had all the negatives for *Never* developed and printed. I married the soundtrack material and had all the raw footage ready for screening.

"Feel like some time travel?" I asked Artie over the phone.

"Huh?" I asked him to meet me for lunch and more details.

We met at Musso and Frank's Grill. I hadn't seen Artie in person since '74. He was the big success story of our group. He'd been DP on a long list of important movies, and his book, *Modern Fundamentals of Movie Cinematography*, was a film-school staple. As I would in the 1990s and 2000s, he taught at UCLA.

Artie was bald and trim. He looked good. I felt like a sad sack of shit next to him, but I put on my good face. We got caught up, bitched about the current state of the film industry, gossiped about old friends and lingered over our meal.

Over coffee, I sprung the news. "You remember *Never Odd or Even*? From a million years ago?"

"With Sam?"

"Want to see it? I had it all printed . . ."

"Sure." He sounded a little worried. Then he brightened. "*Sure!* When?"

"I can set up a screening anytime this week. What works for you?"

2 PM the next day worked for him. I booked a screening room at UCLA. The scenes were assembled in the order they'd been shot. I felt nervous about seeing this stuff. What if it sucked? The only person I felt comfortable sharing these baby steps with was Artie.

The first sequence was the only one we'd screened, 16 years back. The black and white nighttime visuals still looked great. Artie's control of hand-held camera was impressive. And Sam, just being himself on-screen, brought back memories. Me on-screen, not so hot. I looked fussy and self-conscious.

I remembered that this was back when I had both feet. I missed my right foot more than I realized, and as I watched, I choked back tears—for the sight of Sam and the knowledge that the me on the screen had no idea he was about to lose that foot. He just took that foot for granted, like his good health.

Artie and I both chuckled at the real-life accident that became part of the scene—and Sam's on-camera pickpocketing. The scene wasn't going anywhere before that drunk drove into the light-post. The wrap-up to the scene was darkly funny. It was better than I remembered—its success due in no small part to Artie's agile camera-eye.

Next was the scene where Sam, Charlotte and I planned the bank robbery. We were all into our characters, and Artie enhanced the scene by circling the table, his camera tight on our heads and shoulders. The camera's presence felt like an interrogator.

Sam was all business and dominated the scene with his intensity. Charlotte provided some comedy relief and, in her few lines of spontaneous dialogue, a slight sexual charge. I looked tense, shifty, uncertain. The overall effect was like a documentary, and the scene had a grainy, gritty look with the fluctuating motel light bouncing off the walls and the white of our shirts. I spotted Owen in the background once, holding his microphone in the air. That little portable recorder did a good job of capturing the dialogue.

The next bit was the earlier scene of our entry to First City Savings and Loan. Artie had a wide-angle lens for this scene, and it made the dowdy little bank seem cavernous. With the subdued lighting, the scene was murky, but the contrast could be punched up in the lab.

I'd forgotten about the "Mr. Finkel is a goose" sign. Artie and I both cracked up at that—and at Sam eating the leftover sandwich someone had left on the counter. Charlotte was a little over the top in her performance. This was before she'd gotten into the character.

It was a 10-minute scene, full of detail as we discovered all the crap behind the counter, with Artie's camera trailing us after it made a visually satisfying sweep of the rows of barred windows outside the teller cages.

Sam's discovery of the cash, and his on-screen robbery, was funny and shocking. In character as himself, he did what the situation called for. His matter-of-fact demeanor gave way to glee when he realized he—*we*—would get away with this crime. The lights came up. The Albany bank robbery was on another reel. I needed to pee, and Artie tagged along.

At one urinal, I asked: "So. Thoughts? Reactions?"

Artie, from his pissoir: "You know, it's not bad. Given that we were a bunch of kids who didn't really know what we were doing."

"Sam was such a natural. So good on camera."

"Well, his character wasn't much of a stretch, you know?" Artie laughed. "What a *rascal*. I can't believe we took that money."

"But ya *did*, Artie, ya *did*," I said, in an attempt at a Bette Davis accent. We both laughed.

"I'm kind of excited to see the Albany stuff. Just to see if that suitcase camera worked."

"I still can't believe we got away with having a camera right there." I finished, waggled and flushed.

"It's great to finally see this stuff," I said over the sink as I washed my hands.

"Sure brings back memories."

"I miss working with you. We should get together on a project sometime."

"I wouldn't mind that at all."

"Well, let's see the big scene." I felt nervous. After all this time of imagining what it might look like, we were about to be confronted with what was there on film.

I tapped on the projection room door. "Roll that second reel, please." I heard the machine come to life and heard the aperture plate click. Raw leader rolled on the screen. With a loud clump on the soundtrack, the reel started with some *Gun Crazy*-style backseat footage. Sam and Charlotte were in the front seat. Artie had almost no elbow room with Owen and I beside him, but he kept the camera steady.

Incoming wind from the front of the car muddled the soundtrack, but the footage was great—my tribute to the eccentric movie that inspired this whole effort.

The car arced into a parking space and shuddered to a camera-shaking stop. Artie's camera eased out of the back seat and followed Sam and Charlotte to the front of the car. They talked, but Owen was still inside the car, so the soundtrack was a muffle of street sounds.

We cut to the interior of the bank. "Oh, *no*," Artie said. The suitcase-cam's peephole wasn't quite big enough for the lens. The scene had a fuzzy aura around its edges.

"Like a silent movie," I said. "Those iris shots they used to do."

"I *guess*." Once we got used to this fringe around the picture, the image and sound quality was pretty good. The camera inevitably shook from time to time, but the visuals were sharply focused. Owen got a great cavernous sound of the goings-on in the bank.

To the left of center-frame, Sam stood, his back to the camera. He looked over his shoulder once or twice as he advanced in line. Artie panned over to Charlotte and the guard.

"I wish we'd been able to get a couple of close-ups of those two."

"Yeah. It's a miracle we got this shot."

Sam advanced to the head of the line. He looked towards Clarence, the harmless guard, then to his left, in case the FBI chose that moment to rush through the main entrance.

The transaction had no drama. You had to know Sam was robbing the bank for it to have much impact. I was surprised by the robbery's calm. The teller held a poker face, handed over the cash, gave a business-like smile, and Sam exited out the door and up the stairs to his escape.

Jostled, blurred footage followed as Artie darted out the front and around the bank building. He got the camera stabilized just in time to catch Sam walking fast into the alleyway.

This was silent footage. But it was fine. *Bam!* Sam slung the bag of loot under the car. Artie got a great centered shot. The movement had now forced the lens through the peephole, so the fuzz-iris was gone. Sam walked quick and calm, hands in pockets. Artie got a beautiful shot of him in the alleyway. The camera moved in sync with Sam's steps. It was like something out of Max Ophuls.

Sam waited for the street to clear, then made a diagonal for the movie theater. He paid for a ticket, looked over his shoulder, and entered the theater. Artie held the shot for about a minute, as if he expected the Keystone Kops to burst into frame. Nothing happened. Trucks and busses whizzed by. Artie panned up to the theater's marquee as the magazine of film ran out.

The end of the reel was a series of wild shots—scenes of Sam, Charlotte, Owen and me. Artie got a good shot of us standing in the lot of the Pay-Day Motel, talking about something in the sunlight. Bits and pieces of driving, hanging out in the rooms, a shot of Sam passed out asleep on a bed, moments of me hobbling on my umbrella-cane.

"How did you get this stuff?"

"Ends of reels. There was some un-shot film, and I hated to waste it . . ."

"God bless you, Artie."

The reel ran out. The screen bathed us in blinding white until the projectionist shut off the lamp.

I waited for the reels to be rewound. "Well," I said.

"It was better than I expected," Artie said. "Too bad we couldn't *finish* it. It definitely needs . . ."

"More of a *story*. There's not enough to make a coherent movie here."

"What will you *do* with this?"

"Not sure. I need to sleep on it." I heard the *flaplaplaplaplap* that meant the reel was rewound. The projectionist bounded down the stairs with the film cans. I gave him a 20 and thanked him.

"Well," Artie said as we entered the sunlight, squinting like moles.

"I'm starting to put a new picture together. If you're available, I'd love to work with you again. See what we've both learned over the years."

"I'll check my calendar and call you. Be great to team up again, Charlie." We shook hands.

I started to walk away with the film cans. "*Thank* you. It made my day to finally see that stuff."

2

I slept on it for another 20 years. Artie and I did two more pictures together—a drama about a broke young couple in a small town called *Blues of a Lifetime* and a caper film, shot during my brief indie-cinema resurgence, titled *12:04*.

During both shoots, it felt like we were in our 20s again, making movies without frills, storyboarded and pre-prepared but loose and open to whim and experimentation.

Neither film attracted much attention, beyond some kind reviews from longtime advocates of my stuff. These were small films, destined for brief art house runs and a longer life on the shelves of video shops (remember them?) where they finally broke even, or realized a small profit.

By 2000, the writing was on the wall. There was limited room for the kind of movies I wanted to make, and younger, hipper directors elbowed their way to the front of the line. The praise from Tarantino and a couple of other young directors gave me a lifeline for a while.

Through the first decade of this new century, I made three films. It usually took two years between each new project—to put the basic idea together and to get someone to sign off on it. I wasn't a big name. I'd not become a Sid Lumet or a Marty Ritt. After years of grinding away, making the movies I wanted to make, with occasional compromises, I was, at best, a minor figure on the film scene. I had a small following, but there was never a line around the block for any of my movies after *Summer and Sandy*.

In 2011, I called Artie out of the blue with an idea. He was semi-retired, and sick of the grind. "What if we made a documentary out of *Never Odd or Even*? Took the footage and narrated it. Talked about what it was like making this experiment. And finally told the truth about Sam?"

"*Huh*," Artie said. It was an intrigued "*huh*."

"I think the statute of limitations is in our favor. They couldn't prosecute us for those robberies."

"You want to *check* on that? Then call me back."

Thanks to the Internet, I had an answer within an hour. The federal statute was five years. Neither of the banks we'd robbed still legally existed. First City Savings & Loan was closed in 1988, after a string of lawsuits and charges of criminal negligence. The Albany bank had been absorbed into a national chain that went belly-up during The Great Recession.

"I think we're safe, Artie."

"Well, let's do this."

We had a series of on-camera conversations about the project— recorded on digital, so we could ramble to our heart's content without worry of the film running out.

That formed the core of the film-about-a-film. I did some solo talking about my student films, and how *Racecar*'s success got me into a position where I could make a professional movie. Talked about the novel, and about the influences that led me down the path I chose as a film-maker.

And I got Charlotte, after much heel-dragging, to sit with me and talk about her relationship with Sam, about her reservations about being filmed in compromising positions. "I lived in fear that the footage of that robbery would show up sometime. Thank you for sitting on it for so long. I'm at the point where a little larceny won't affect my career one way or another!"

Then I found Owen Schiff. He had moved from one corner of paradise to another. He lived and worked in Key West, where he earned his keep taking tourists out on day-long sailing trips. He was shocked to hear from me. "I guess I thought you were dead," he said.

I couldn't convince him to leave Key West, so I went to him, parked my digicam on the deck of his boat, and we talked *Never Odd or Even* (and *Summer and Sandy*) against the stunning backdrop of the true-blue sky and the ocean.

Owen told the story of his last days with Sam for the record. I realized that Charlotte and Artie had skirted this subject, and I returned to LA eager to get them to release this ancient cat from its musty bag.

The three of us sat on my back porch, with its hazy view of the Hollywood hills, and revealed the hoax of Sam-as-expat poet. The three of us corrected one another and got the whole story on digital video for the record. This was the story that *Never Odd or Even* needed.

I spent the next two and a half years editing *Never Odd or Even: The Film That Never Was*. The first cut ran over four hours. I knew no one would have a fraction of the patience for such an endurance test. I kept that version for myself. I've watched it many times.

Cutting the story down to two hours—including generous samples of the *film maudit*—was the toughest work I've ever done as a film-maker. I subjected Artie to several cuts of the film, and his advice gave me a rudder. I got what felt like the right balance of the story behind the film and sequences from the film itself—with the story of *Summer and Sandy* another strong current in the narrative.

The story of Barrett Broadford has already been covered in documentaries, so I'm afraid he got short shrift in my film. He never wrote another screenplay after *Summer and Sandy*. He tried, but success, and the pressure to come up with something as good as, if not better than, his first effort wrecked him. The income from his one film kept him going, on a subsistence level, but the harder he tried to create another scenario, the deeper he got into creative impotence. The story of his suicide didn't surprise me when it made the papers. I wish I could have done something to help him.

3

It took a couple of years, but the documentary made the film-festival rounds. To my, Artie and Charlotte's surprise, it generated good buzz. The story of a group of young renegade filmmakers making a made-up movie in secret—which sat on a shelf for close to 40 years—spoke to a new generation of cinema fans. And filmmakers.

At one screening, a young director said he admired our courage in taking this huge risk. "But the hardest part must have been sitting on this for so long." The audience gave mild applause for this statement.

"Well, I kept busy. You know, I managed to make a lot of movies. I was lucky. Aside from *Sandy*, I never delivered a blockbuster. I'm not a big name. And that's given me the freedom to make movies I wanted to make, and that I hoped people would want to see. What other reason is there to go through all this trouble?"

The film got a theatrical run, distributed by Miramax, and earned a Best Documentary nomination—another near-miss at the golden statuette. I was interviewed by *Sight and Sound* and *Film Comment*, and a reappraisal of my work happened. I was considered, in the words of *Sight and Sound*'s critic, ". . . the best-kept open secret of the American cinema as its sights shifted from art to commerce." I can't take that credit, but it was nice of the guy to say.

I've toured the art house circuit as some of my early films were restored. *No Room at The Royal* found an eager audience and The Criterion Collection put it out on DVD and BluRay. I was wined and dined by younger film fans and directors, some who said our guerilla approach on *Never* inspired them to go out with their digital equipment and try to get something real into their work. They work with equipment they can carry in their pockets. They've never cut a negative or schlepped a can of 35mm film up several flights of stairs. Those days are gone.

I got Artie and Charlotte to accompany me on some of these junkets. Charlotte is a riot with a live audience. They recognize her from all the crap TV she's done and are surprised by her wit and candor.

Owen couldn't be reached; he must have changed his number. Maybe he didn't want to be in the public eye. I had to respect his wishes, but he deserved acclaim for what he'd done with us.

Summer and Sandy remains the movie I'm best-known for. It's never lost its effect of the young and the naïve. I am pleased that some of my later movies—which I think knock *Sandy* out of the running—are available for streaming online.

The world moves on, and any film pre-*Star Wars* is eyed with suspicion by many younger viewers. Outside of Turner Classic Movies, you don't see pre-1980s films on television anymore.

Everything becomes obsolete. The Glenn Miller Orchestra was as big as The Beatles in its day. It carried some cachet into the 1970s, but once its target audience started dying off, and radio stations stopped playing music from that era, it vanished from the horizon. The same thing will happen with The Beatles someday.

Fewer new movies speak to me each year. I haven't seen a franchise movie—or anything with a number at the end of its title—since the early 2000s. Life's too short.

My favorite movie of this millennium, to date, is *The Florida Project*. Here was some of the spirit of *Los Olvidados* back on the screen—with a touch of those early, crude "Our Gang" talkies. The movie's unflinching eye, its fearless view of human tragedy: it resonated with me, and with what I've tried to do in my film-making career. Even if there's just one movie a year like this one, that means the spirit of meaningful motion pictures will stay alive and well.

4

In 2020, during lockdown, I was bored out of my gourd. I did some Zoom interviews, but that only spun my wheels. I needed to make another movie. Aside from the documentary, I hadn't released a new film since 2009. Maybe this would be my last one. Hell, Eastwood's still directing, and he's got some years on me.

One afternoon, I got a flash: I could make a for-real version of *Never Odd or Even*. Set it in the present, with unknowns. Go on the road with the same idea we used, let the cast decide where to take the story and their characters, and make a nice cameo for Charlotte.

I cold-called Artie, stuck in place in Beverly Hills and antsy as I. "They'll figure out a vaccine for this bug, you know? Just like polio. And the world will want new movies. I think the basic idea still works, and to do it now . . . we could show how the world has changed, and that crime adapts to the times.

"You and me, just like 1962. Let the chips fall where they may."

"Huh," Artie said with intrigue. "*Huh*." I felt giddy with the notion. "You know . . . I'd like that. I'm sick of green screens, blue screens . . . *any* color screens. I don't like how movies are just . . .

assembled. Like a dishwasher. I'd love to get my feet on the ground. Hold a camera in my hands. Be in a real place with real people."

"Yes!"

Nothing went forward for a year, as the world took baby steps towards whatever passed for normal. Cut to late spring, 2021. I've made some good friends with young directors: they see me as a mentor and I'm glad to offer my experience as it relates to the future of movies.

In turn, they've made me aware of the rich potential of TV series. I had one terrible experience with network TV in 1971. I was asked to turn Joan Didion's collection of essays about the hippie culture of Haight-Ashbury into a cautionary, episodic soap opera. I hated doing it and I never saw the finished version after ABC took out anything they felt objectionable. Didion's estate barred it from being shown again. For that, I thank them every day.

I never could sit and look at TV. I thought it a wasteland. I was wrong; I was glad to be aware of its new possibilities.

"It's a bigger canvas," Griffin, a mentee of mine, explained. "It's like a movie that has more time for the little moments. You do it in little 50-minute chunks, but you can explore every character . . . it's more like reading a novel. Each episode's, like, a chapter."

Griffin is into low-budget psychological horror, but he knows from movies. He gave me a list of series to watch, from *The Walking Dead* to *The White Lotus*. Some I didn't like, but I got it. This had the breathing room I never knew I needed.

Artie loved the idea of doing our story as a series. He knew someone at Showtime and got us a Zoom pitch with a kid who'd seen the documentary and loved our idea. That's as far as it's gotten. Artie and I have a lot to work out. He loves this part; getting ducks in a row is his great joy. I still suffer through it. It's necessary evil defined.

This just might turn into something. I'm too used to hearing the word *no* to turn cartwheels. (They'd be slow cartwheels.) There's real promise in this project, and if it gets made, Artie and I are gonna have a ball. Watch this space.

THE END

FILM NOIR CLASSICS

THE PITFALL Jay Dratler
"Dratler's novel is darker, sleazier and less forgiving than the film it inspired. A brutal portrait of blind lust and self-destruction..." —Cullen Gallagher, *Pulp Serenade*. Filmed in 1948 with Dick Powell, Lizabeth Scott, Jane Wyatt and Raymond Burr.

FALLEN ANGEL Marty Holland
"This story, about a small-time grifter who lands in a central California town and hooks up with a femme fatale, is straight out of the James M. Cain playbook."—Bill Ott, *Booklist*. Filmed in 1945 with Dana Andrews, Alice Faye and Linda Darnell.

THE VELVET FLEECE
Lois Eby & John C. Fleming
"We guarantee your head will be spinning with double-crosses and you'll be talking out of both sides of your mouth before you finish...." —*Evening Star*.
Filmed as *Larceny* in 1948 starring John Payne, Joan Caulfield and Dan Duryea.

SUDDEN FEAR Edna Sherry
"This is a thoroughly exciting read, with brilliant pacing, which makes you absolutely desperate to know how everything will pan out."—Kate Jackson. Filmed in 1952 with Joan Crawford, Jack Palance and Gloria Grahame.

HOLLOW TRIUMPH Murray Forbes
"...a disturbed personality done in the noir tradition... an atmospheric and evocative yarn that spans the late 30s to through WWII."—Amazon reader. Filmed in 1948 with Paul Henreid and Joan Bennett as *The Scar*.

THE DARK CORNER /
SLEEP, MY LOVE Leo Rosten
"The slang is tangy, the plots magnetic, the suspense sweet, the hilarity edgy... For all lovers of vintage noir."
—Donna Seaman, *Booklist*. Filmed in 1946 and 1948 with Lucille Ball, Clifton Well, Claudette Colbert and Robert Cummings.

DEADLIER THAN THE MALE
James Gunn
"The attitude of the book... reels between black comedy and surrealism drenched in a misanthropy that is occasionally stunning."
—Ed Gorman. Filmed as *Born to Kill* in 1947 with Lawrence Tierney and Claire Trevor.

KISS THE BLOOD OFF MY HANDS
Gerald Butler
"The violence, crime, brutality, and 'trapped-in-a-narrow-place' aspects of noir are all here."—Carl Waluconis. Filmed in 1948 with Joan Fontaine and Burt Lancaster.

MOONRISE Theodore Strauss
"Moonrise is unique in that it's one of the few noirs in which the redemptive power of love holds nihilism at bay."—Eddie Muller. Filmed in 1948 with Dane Clark and Gail Russell.

Mad With Much Heart — Gerald Butler
"This is a page turner in the true sense of the word, starting with a car chase and culminating with a hazardous race up the side of a snow-covered hill."—Ron Koltnow. Filmed in 1951 by Nicholas Ray as *On Dangerous Ground* with Robert Ryan and Ida Lupino.

In trade paperback from...
Stark House Press, 1315 H Street, Eureka, CA 95501
greg@starkhousepress.com / www.StarkHousePress.com
Available from your local bookstore, or order direct via our website.